FRIGHTMARES™

Don't Go
Near
Mrs. Tallie

Books by Peg Kehret

Cages
Horror at the Haunted House
Nightmare Mountain
Sisters, Long Ago
Terror at the Zoo
Frightmares™: Cat Burglar on the Prowl
Frightmares™: Bone Breath and the Vandals
Frightmares™: Don't Go Near Mrs. Tallie

Available from MINSTREL Books

FRIGHTMARES™

Don't Go Near Mrs. Tallie

Peg Kehret

For the students at NIK

Peg Kehret

A MINSTREL® HARDCOVER
PUBLISHED BY POCKET BOOKS

New York   London   Toronto   Sydney   Tokyo   Singapore

A MINSTREL HARDCOVER

A Minstrel Book published by
POCKET BOOKS, a division of Simon & Schuster Inc.
1230 Avenue of the Americas, New York, NY 10020

Kehret, Peg.
    Don't go near Mrs. Tallie / Peg Kehret.
        p.   cm. — (Frightmares: #3)
    "A Minstrel hardcover."
    Summary: While trying to find a new home for Mrs. Tallie's cat,
Care Club members Rosie and Kayo discover that their elderly
neighbor may be the victim of a horrifying plot to do her harm.
    ISBN 0-671-89192-8
    [1. Clubs—Fiction.   2. Cats—Fiction.   3. Mystery and detective
stories.]   I. Title.   II. Series: Kehret, Peg. Frightmares: #3.
PZ7.K2518Do   1995
[Fic]—dc20   94-42090
                                                             CIP
                                                              AC

First Minstrel Books hardcover printing August 1995

10 9 8 7 6 5 4 3 2 1

FRIGHTMARES is a trademark of Simon & Schuster Inc.

A MINSTREL BOOK and colophon are registered trademarks of
Simon & Schuster Inc.

Printed in the U.S.A.

For Willo Davis Roberts,
who inspired and encouraged me

CARE CLUB
We Care About Animals

I. Whereas we, the undersigned, care about our animal friends, we promise to groom them, play with them, and exercise them daily. We will do this for the following animals:

> **WEBSTER** (Rosie's cat)
> **BONE BREATH** (Rosie's dog)
> **HOMER** (Kayo's cat)
> **DIAMOND** (Kayo's cat)

II. Whereas we, the undersigned, care about the well-being of *all* creatures, we promise to do whatever we can to help homeless animals.

III. Care Club will hold official meetings every Thursday afternoon or whenever else there is important business. All Care Club projects will be for the good of the animals.

Signed:

Rosie Saunders

Kayo Benton

FRIGHTMARES™

Don't Go
Near
Mrs. Tallie

Chapter

Extra Credit Report
Mrs. Cushman's 6th Grade Class

CARE CLUB'S GREAT DISASTER

By Rosie Saunders

Here is what happened last week:

A. I almost got murdered.

B. I helped the police catch an unscrupulous criminal.

C. I saved a cat's life.

D. I discovered a poisonous plant.

E. I received the stupidest poem in the world from a certain wallydraigle in my

1

class who should give up writing poetry
forever.

*M*y dad says it was Care Club's Great Disaster.
My mom refuses to discuss it except to say she
did not expect raising a child to give her
frightmares, which are even worse than night-
mares, but I manage to do it on a regular basis.

Now that the great disaster is over, I'm glad I
met Mrs. Tallie. At the time—well, I admit that
at the time I was scared stiff. So was my friend,
Kayo Benton, who is the other half of Care Club
and who did all of the above with me.

Chapter

"Don't go near Mrs. Tallie. This is a warning: *Stay away from her!*"

Rosie Saunders gripped the telephone, her lips parted in surprise. The voice sounded nasal, as if the speaker had a head cold or was pinching his nose together while he spoke.

"If you go there again," the caller said, "you will be sorry. Very sorry." He spoke slowly, pausing slightly between each word.

The threatening words made Rosie's skin crawl.

"Who is this?" Rosie said.

"Don't go near Mrs. Tallie," the voice repeated. "Keep your friend away, too. And don't tell anyone about this call."

"You have the wrong number," Rosie said.

"No, Rosie. The warning is for you, and for your friend. Stay away—or suffer."

Rosie hung up. Trembling, she remained next to the telephone, wondering if it would ring again.

Maybe I should not have hung up on him, she thought. Maybe I should have tried to keep him talking to see if I could recognize his voice.

Her parents had told her if she ever got an obscene or threatening phone call to hang up immediately. Chances are, they said, the caller had dialed a number at random and would not ever call again.

This call, Rosie knew, was not a random call. This caller used her name. He had dialed her number on purpose. He knew who she was, and he knew that she and Kayo were helping Mrs. Tallie.

If he knows my name and phone number, Rosie realized, he knows my address, too. He knows where to find me.

She walked to the window and looked out. There were no people in sight but Rosie closed the drapes anyway.

All her life Rosie had felt safe in this house.

Don't Go Near Mrs. Tallie

She loved the large bright rooms, the bay window with its cushioned window seat, the stone fireplace, and the shelves filled with books. But as she stood beside the silent telephone, with the horrible voice echoing in her memory, she was scared.

She was scared for herself, scared for Kayo, and scared for Mrs. Tallie. This warning—this terrible, anonymous phone call—confirmed Rosie's suspicions. We can't stay away, Rosie thought. Not now. We have to help Mrs. Tallie.

Chapter 3

Rosie had met Mrs. Tallie three days before the phone call.

She had been walking her dog, Bone Breath, past a stately old house with beautiful flower gardens. When she paused to sniff the yellow roses that climbed an iron fence around the property, a voice called, "The gate is open. Come in, if you want to smell the roses."

An elderly woman, half hidden behind the roses, beckoned from a small bench. "Your dog has lovely fur," the woman said. "You should make a sweater out of it."

Visions of Bone Breath getting sheared like a sheep flashed through Rosie's head. "Cairn terriers are not supposed to get clipped," she said.

"You don't cut the dog's fur off," Mrs. Tallie said. "You save the loose fur every time you comb or brush him. When you have enough, you wash it, spin it into yarn, and then knit a sweater with the yarn." She put out her hand. "I am Mrs. Tallie," she said.

Rosie shook hands and told her name.

"Do you have a dog?" Rosie asked. Maybe she could see a sweater made of dog fur.

"I have a cat. Muffin. But I've had dogs in the past. Sparky was the best and, yes, I knit a sweater out of his fur." Mrs. Tallie's lined face crinkled even more as she grinned broadly. "I didn't make a sweater for me, though," she said. "I knit a sweater for him. I saved Sparky's fur and knit him a little turtleneck sweater. Every time he wore it, people stopped us on the street and asked about it."

I'll bet they did, Rosie thought.

"Sparky and I worked together in the circus," Mrs. Tallie said. "We rode an elephant. Standing up. I wore tights covered with red sequins, and Sparky wore a ruffled collar that matched. He stood on his hind legs on my shoulders and I stood on the elephant, and we went round and round the circus ring. Oh, it brought them to their feet, clapping, every time."

Usually Rosie's imagination worked overtime, but she had difficulty picturing this frail white-haired woman in red sequined tights, with a dog on her shoulders, riding on an elephant.

Mrs. Tallie peered at Rosie. "How old are you?" she asked.

"Twelve."

"And still living at home, with your parents?" She said it as if Rosie were forty, not twelve.

"I'm in sixth grade," Rosie said. Her round glasses slipped down her nose, and she shoved them back with one finger. "I'll live with my parents at least until I finish high school."

"Ha!" Mrs. Tallie said. "That's the trouble with young people today. No sense of adventure. Why, by the time I was sixteen, I had been chased by a grizzly bear in Alaska, dug up dinosaur bones in Montana, and planted two hundred mango trees in India. Mango trees are sacred there; did you know that?"

"No," said Rosie. "I didn't."

Bone Breath licked Mrs. Tallie's hand; she petted him.

8

Don't Go Near Mrs. Tallie

"Good dog," she said. "Nice dog." Tears sprang to her eyes. "I've loved all my animals," she said softly. "Sparky and FooFoo and all the others—there have been so many dear creatures through the years—and now I have to say goodbye to my last one. My darling Muffin."

"Is your cat sick?" Rosie said.

"She's perfectly healthy."

"I don't understand."

"I can't take care of this property alone any more. All those rooms and this huge yard. Even with a gardener, it's too much for me."

"So you're selling your house?"

"I was going to, until my nephew offered to move in and help me. I want to stay here, in my own home, but Bert is allergic to cat fur. When Bert is in the same room with Muffin, his nose runs, his eyes swell shut, and he gets short of breath. If Muffin rubs against him or he accidentally touches her, it's even worse. So Muffin needs a new home."

They talked a while longer and Mrs. Tallie showed Rosie the other garden areas. Then Rosie hurried home and called her best friend, Kayo Benton. "Get over here right away," she said when Kayo answered.

"I'm making peanut butter cookies."

"Turn off the oven. We need an emergency Care Club meeting."

Ten minutes later Kayo and Rosie sat in Rosie's bedroom. "I could be eating fresh cookies right now," Kayo said. "This had better be a genuine emergency."

"It is." Rosie told her about Mrs. Tallie and Muffin and the allergic nephew.

"Poor old Muffin," Kayo said. "Eleven years of faithful cathood and she gets evicted. It isn't fair. Doesn't Mrs. Tallie have a friend who would take her cat? Then Mrs. Tallie could visit Muffin."

Rosie shook her head. "She said she has no family except Bert, and the only one of her friends who is well enough to care for an animal is her gardener. He doesn't like cats because they dig in his soil."

"She should put a Free Cat ad in the paper. That's how Mom and I got Homer and Diamond."

"Mrs. Tallie is afraid some unscrupulous person might take Muffin." Rosie took her vocabulary notebook out of her pocket and made a check mark beside the word *unscrupulous.*

"Un-what?" said Kayo.

10

"Unscrupulous. It means without moral integrity. No conscience."

"Oh," said Kayo. "A crook."

"Finding a home for Muffin can be an official Care Club project," said Rosie.

"Maybe we should just find someone to adopt Muffin and leave Care Club out of it."

"But this is a perfect Care Club activity," Rosie said. "Our charter says we're supposed to help homeless animals, and Muffin will soon be homeless."

"True," Kayo said. "It's just that every Care Club project we've tried so far has ended with us screaming for help."

"I admit, Care Club has had some unusual adventures," Rosie said.

"Unusual," said Kayo, "spelled S-C-A-R-Y."

"How can we get in trouble by helping Mrs. Tallie find a home for her cat?"

"I don't know," said Kayo. "That's what worries me; I don't know."

"If we're going to be scared to do any more projects," Rosie said, "we may as well not have a club."

Kayo took off her Baltimore Orioles baseball cap, smoothed back her hair, and put the cap on

11

backward. She said, "I move that Care Club find a home for Muffin Tallie."

Rosie smiled. "All those in favor, say aye."

"Aye," said Kayo.

"Aye," said Rosie.

"Opposed?"

Silence.

"The motion carries," said Rosie.

"Here we go again," said Kayo.

Chapter 4

S ix pages," Kayo grumbled. "Mrs. Cushman thinks there is nothing in our lives except spare time in which to do massive amounts of homework."

The girls were on their way to Mrs. Tallie's house so Kayo could meet Muffin. "How are we going to write six-page science reports?" Kayo continued. "Did you know there are twenty-eight lines on a piece of notebook paper? I counted last night. Even if I leave the last three lines of each page blank, for a bottom margin, that still leaves twenty-five lines per page to write on. Twenty-five lines times six pages, is one hundred and fifty lines of writing! Why not ask us to write an entire encyclopedia?" She swung an imaginary bat, as if she could knock the science report over the fence and out of her life.

"Mine's half done," Rosie said.

"We only got the assignment yesterday. How can you be half done already?"

Rosie shrugged. "I like to write reports," she said. "It gives me a chance to use my vocabulary words."

"What are you writing about?"

"Pet health hazards. I'm using all the things we learned in our Saturday class."

"Why didn't I think of that?" Kayo said. "You won't have to do any research, and you can put in all that information about how pets die from eating slug bait and antifreeze."

Every Saturday for the last month the girls had attended an Oakwood Parks Department class on Health Care for Domestic Animals. Each class was led by a veterinarian or other pet care professional and covered a different topic. So far, Rosie and Kayo had learned about flea control, proper diet, grooming, health hazards, and common illnesses of dogs, cats, and hamsters.

"Why don't you do your report on one of the other topics we learned about?" Rosie suggested.

"What an All-Star idea," Kayo said. "I can probably fill up six pages on pet nutrition or disease, if I write big." She took another practice swing with her imaginary bat.

"Make a chart about vitamins. Mrs. Cushman loves it when we make charts."

"Did you make a chart?"

"Not yet, but I plan to do one on poisonous plants. I'll copy some of the drawings from that handout we got and label them and color them with my markers. I may have enough for two charts."

"If you have two pages of charts, you'll only have to fill up four pages with writing," Kayo said.

"I'll still write the six pages. The charts will be extra."

"Not me," said Kayo. "Any chart I make will be instead of one page of writing." Kayo wondered how she and Rosie got along so well when they were so different. "I can't believe you *like* to write reports," she said.

"And I can't believe you like to run two miles a day and do sit-ups every night and lift those heavy weights."

"How can I be a professional baseball player if

I don't keep in shape?" Kayo said as she adjusted her Orioles cap.

"Hey!" called a voice behind them.

Turning, the girls saw Sammy Hulenback pedaling toward them on his bicycle.

"Here comes your boyfriend," said Rosie.

"Dream on," said Kayo.

"Not everyone has a wallydraigle in love with her. You should feel flattered."

Kayo giggled. Usually she forgot Rosie's vocabulary words as soon as the week was over, but *wallydraigle*, meaning an imperfect or slovenly person, had become their secret name for Sammy.

Sammy braked to a stop beside them. "Where are you going?" he asked.

"We're on a secret mission for the FBI," Rosie said. "All we can tell you is that it involves lava flows on Mars."

"No way," said Sammy. "What are you really doing?"

"We're helping a cat find a home," Kayo said.

"Which cat?" Sammy asked. "Homer or Diamond?"

"Not my cats," Kayo said. "Mrs. Tallie's cat." She pointed ahead at Mrs. Tallie's house.

16

"Maybe I can take it," Sammy said.

Kayo and Rosie looked at each other in alarm.

"Do you still have your Saint Bernard?" Rosie asked.

"Yes."

"Napoleon's awfully big," Kayo said. "Muffin would be scared of him."

"Maybe not," said Sammy. "What are you guys writing your science reports on?"

"Warm-blooded dinosaurs," said Kayo.

Sammy scowled, as if unsure whether to believe her or not. "Dinosaurs were cold-blooded," he said.

"New research about the amount of oxygen in dinosaur bones shows they may have been warm-blooded." Unfortunately, Kayo thought, there wasn't enough research to fill six pages.

"I'm writing mine on tapeworms," Sammy said.

"Yuck," said Rosie.

"Strike one," said Kayo.

"I found what looked like pieces of dried-up rice on Napoleon's back leg," Sammy said. "The vet said they were tapeworm segments."

"Gross," said Kayo. "Spare us the details, please."

"I still have the pieces of tapeworm," Sammy said.

"You kept them?" said Kayo.

"I'm going to glue them on my report."

"Strike two," said Kayo.

"That is the most disgusting thing I ever heard," said Rosie.

"You could do your report on tapeworms, too," said Sammy. "We can write them together. I'll even give you one of the pieces of tapeworm."

"Strike three," said Kayo. "Goodbye."

"I'll go ask my mom if I can have a cat." Sammy rode off.

"I wish he would catch on that you are never going to be his girlfriend," Rosie said, "and quit pestering us."

"Sammy is the last person in the whole world I would give Muffin to," said Kayo as they watched him pedal away.

"It would be unscrupulous to give Muffin to that wallydraigle," said Rosie. Smiling, she took out her vocabulary notebook and made a check. "Two in one sentence," she said. "Not bad."

Kayo tried to remember what *unscrupulous* meant. "Do you think Sammy's a crook?" she asked.

"*We* would be unscrupulous if we gave Muffin to a dim bulb like Sammy who has a Saint Bernard." Rosie pushed open Mrs. Tallie's gate and the girls stepped inside.

"Wow," said Kayo as they followed a path through a jumble of pink and red roses. "This place is like the houses in my mom's magazines."

"You are trespassing." The deep voice behind them made both girls jump. They turned and saw a gray-haired man wearing tan coveralls and cotton garden gloves striding toward them. He carried a pair of small pruning shears. "What are you doing here?" he demanded.

"We're Rosie Saunders and Kayo Benton," Rosie said. "We are finding a new home for Mrs. Tallie's cat. Are you Bert?"

"I am Mr. Cookson, the gardener. You don't need to bother about that cat. It leaves tomorrow."

"You found someone to take Muffin?" Rosie was torn between relief that Muffin had a new home and disappointment that Care Club was not responsible for finding it.

"Tomorrow," he said, "I am taking that cat to the animal shelter."

"Tomorrow!" Kayo cried. "That doesn't give us much time to find Muffin a new home."

"It's none too soon, if you ask me. That fool cat has been digging in my garden for years, but Mrs. Tallie is so attached to the silly creature that it took a full-blown medical crisis this afternoon to convince her to get rid of it."

"What happened?" Rosie asked.

"Bert was asleep on the sofa. The fool cat crept in and laid on Bert's chest and rubbed her head under Bert's chin. Bert dreamed he was suffocating, and when he woke up, he nearly was. That's when Mrs. Tallie realized she can't put it off any longer. The cat has to go."

"Hello. I thought I heard voices." Mrs. Tallie came down the path, leaning on a cane.

After Rosie introduced Kayo, Mrs. Tallie insisted they go inside for a glass of milk and an oatmeal cookie. "Will you join us, Mr. Cookson?" she asked.

"I'm clipping the old roses," Mr. Cookson said.

Kayo was glad. She didn't care much for the gardener who was so eager to get rid of Mrs. Tallie's pet.

The girls followed Mrs. Tallie through the back door into the kitchen. It was a large room containing a round oak table and six wooden chairs. The carved table legs looked like a lion's feet, complete with claws. Mrs. Tallie motioned for the girls to sit down.

"Bert!" she called. "We have guests."

A thin, pale young man, not much taller than Kayo, entered the kitchen. He smiled and shook hands with Rosie and Kayo, then bustled about putting cookies on a plate.

Mrs. Tallie picked up a teakettle and began filling it with water.

Bert said, "Sit down and rest, Aunt Hilda. I'll fix your tea."

Mrs. Tallie thanked him and eased herself into one of the chairs. "I haven't been well the last few days," she told the girls. "I tire easily and my stomach gets upset when I eat."

"Did you go to your doctor?" Rosie asked.

Mrs. Tallie shook her head. "I'm not one for doctors," she said. "I've seen too many cases where the cure was worse than the disease. I prefer to eat my greens and drink my herbal tea and stay as far away from doctors as I can."

Bert put out a plate of cookies, milk for the girls, and cups of tea for himself and Mrs. Tallie. Kayo thought that, except for his allergy to cats, Bert was the perfect companion for his aunt.

Mrs. Tallie's hand shook when she lifted the

teacup. She nibbled the edge of a cookie and then put it down. "I'm so fortunate that Bert found me after all these years," she said. "I didn't know I had a nephew until his letter came last month. I thought I had no family left at all. Now here he is, cooking and waiting on me as if I were the Queen of England. I feel lazy and spoiled."

"You rest all you need," Bert said, "and get your strength back."

Muffin came into the room and rubbed against Mrs. Tallie's ankles. "Hello, precious pussycat," Mrs. Tallie said. She leaned down to pet the cat.

Muffin purred.

Bert jumped to his feet. "Please excuse me," he said and quickly left the room.

"Oh!" Kayo cried when she saw the cat. "She's adorable! How can you bear to give her up?"

"She is pretty, isn't she?" Mrs. Tallie said. "Did you notice, she has her initial on her forehead?" She pointed to the letter *M* formed from black stripes on Muffin's tan fur. "And she's such a sweet cat."

Muffin jumped on Mrs. Tallie's lap and purred louder. "My good, dear Muffin," Mrs. Tallie murmured. "I'll miss you so." Her eyes filled with tears. "Bert called several veterinary offices," she said, "to see if they knew of anyone who might want a cat, and they all said the same thing. No one wants to adopt an eleven-year-old cat."

"Poor Muffin," Rosie said.

"I had so hoped I could find her a loving home. I don't want to take her to the animal shelter," Mrs. Tallie said. "Muffin won't understand why she is locked in a cage. She'll be unhappy and afraid. And the woman I talked to there said the chances of a cat this old being adopted are slim." She wiped her eyes. "But a slim chance is better than none."

"Care Club will find Muffin a home," Kayo declared.

"Before tomorrow," Rosie said.

"Oh, I do hope so," Mrs. Tallie said.

The girls finished their snack and hurried to Kayo's apartment.

As soon as her mother got home, Kayo said, "I've been offered a free cat. Her name is Muffin and she's eleven and she has her initial on her head. Is it okay with you?"

Mrs. Benton said, "There is no such thing as a free cat. Cat food and litter are not free. Veterinary care is certainly not free, and a cat that age might need medical attention more often than

Homer and Diamond do. The last time they went in for vaccinations, it cost nearly one hundred dollars. A third cat is out of the question."

"Could we keep her temporarily?" Kayo said. "Just until we find someone to take her permanently? It's a Care Club project."

Mrs. Benton shook her head. "I'm sorry, Kayo. We both know that if we took in another cat, neither of us would be able to part with it. We'd be far too attached to ever give it up." She sighed and turned away from the girls. "We cannot afford a third cat," she said, and Kayo knew the discussion was over.

She also knew it wasn't her mom's fault that they were always short of money. Mrs. Benton worked hard at her secretarial job, and she earned a little extra by directing a church choir, but in spite of her efforts, they had to count every nickel. Especially at the end of the month.

If my dad would send support money like he's supposed to, Kayo thought, *we wouldn't be so broke all the time.* But there wasn't anything Kayo could do about that.

When the girls got to Rosie's house, her mother was still at work. Mr. Saunders was in the

Don't Go Near Mrs. Tallie

kitchen making himself a peanut-butter-and-pickle sandwich. Bone Breath sat at his feet, hoping for a bite. Rosie told her dad about Muffin and how Mrs. Tallie had to give her up.

"Now, that's a tear-jerker story, if I ever heard one," Mr. Saunders said. "A real *cata*strophe."

Rosie ignored his pun. "Can we adopt Muffin?" she said. "Please?"

"What about Webster and Bone Breath?" Mr. Saunders said. "They might not like another animal in the house."

When Bone Breath heard his name, he wagged his tail and pawed at Mr. Saunders's foot. Mr. Saunders gave him a piece of bread crust.

"Webster and Bone Breath get along with each other. Why wouldn't they like a new cat?" Rosie said.

"You can try it," Mr. Saunders said. "But I can't be interrupted all day to break up cat fights. If the new one doesn't get along with Webster and Bone Breath, it has to go."

"Thanks, Dad," Rosie said. "You've made an old woman very happy."

"Two young women seem pretty happy, too," said Mr. Saunders as Rosie and Kayo dashed out the door to tell Mrs. Tallie the good news.

25

An hour later they returned, with Muffin in a carrier.

Webster and Bone Breath did not think a new cat was a good idea. When Webster saw Muffin, his fur stood on end, his back arched, and a low, ominous growl rumbled in his throat. Bone Breath ran in circles, barking wildly, which made Muffin cower in terror.

"Keep them separated for a day or two," Mr. Saunders advised. "Let them get used to each other's scent."

Rosie carried Muffin into her bedroom and shut the door. Webster lay on the floor in the hallway and stuck his paw under Rosie's door, rattling it. Bone Breath sat outside the door and whined. When the girls opened the cat carrier, Muffin ran under Rosie's bed and refused to come out.

"This may not be as easy as we thought," Rosie said.

$\mathcal{A}$unt Hilda is too ill for visitors," Bert said, "but since she's worried about Muffin, you can see her for a few minutes. It will ease her mind." He led the girls into the living room, where Mrs. Tallie lay on the sofa, covered with a patchwork quilt.

Rosie and Kayo tried not to show how shocked they were by her appearance. Two days ago Mrs. Tallie was smelling the roses and talking about riding an elephant. Now she could barely wave a greeting. Her eyes were ringed with blue-black circles, as if she hadn't slept in weeks.

Mrs. Tallie motioned for Rosie and Kayo to come closer. When they were directly beside her, she put a finger to her lips, signaling them to be quiet. She raised her head enough to pull the pillow out and began to remove the pillowcase.

Kayo helped her. When the pillowcase was off, Mrs. Tallie unzipped the pillow cover that encased the pillow itself. She reached inside and withdrew a sealed envelope. She handed the envelope to Rosie.

Rosie recognized the address of a downtown building. Her mother's law firm was on the sixth floor of the same building. Mrs. Tallie's letter was addressed to someone on the tenth floor.

"Mail this," Mrs. Tallie whispered. "Don't tell anyone." Exhausted, she sank back on the bed.

Kayo zipped the pillow cover, put the pillowcase back on, and gently lifted Mrs. Tallie's head far enough to put the pillow under it.

Rosie slipped the envelope under her sweatshirt, holding it in place with her elbow so it wouldn't drop out. "Muffin misses you," she said. "I let her sleep on my bed last night."

Mrs. Tallie smiled gratefully. "You're good girls," she said. "You're kind to the animals."

"Is there anything else we can do for you?" Kayo asked.

Don't Go Near Mrs. Tallie

Mrs. Tallie did not reply. She closed her eyes; her breathing sounded shallow and irregular.

"She's asleep," Kayo whispered.

Rosie nodded.

As they tiptoed from the room, Bert came out of the kitchen and walked with them to the door.

"What's wrong with her?" Rosie asked.

"Old age," Bert said. "Aunt Hilda is nearly ninety."

On their way to Kayo's baseball game, the girls dropped the envelope in a mailbox.

"I wonder why she was so secretive about the letter," Rosie said.

"Maybe she's arranging a surprise for Bert, to thank him for taking care of her."

"Maybe," Rosie said. "But something doesn't seem quite right. Mrs. Tallie was nearly ninety last week, too, and she wasn't sick then."

"I can't keep Muffin much longer," Rosie told Kayo on Saturday as they rode the bus to their Animal Care class. "I don't think she'll ever adjust to Bone Breath and Webster. All she does is hide under my bed and meow."

"It's been three days," Kayo said. "I thought by now they would be used to each other."

"So did I. My dad is having a fit. Yesterday, when Mom was at work and I was at school, he couldn't concentrate on his cartoon strips because Muffin kept yowling, which made Bone Breath bark. Dad finally opened my bedroom door, thinking that's what Muffin wanted, but as soon as he did, Bone Breath charged in there and chased Muffin out of the room. Then Webster and Muffin had a big cat fight in the living room, and when Dad tried to break it up, he got bit and scratched and Muffin climbed the drapes and made a huge rip in one of them."

"What are we going to do?"

"I don't know. Mom tried to call Mrs. Tallie last night, but she was too sick to talk."

"We can't take Muffin back to Mrs. Tallie, anyway," Kayo said.

"No, we can't; but I can't keep her, either."

"Let's tell the people in our class about Muffin. Maybe one of them wants a cat."

"If they care about animals enough to come to all these classes, they would give Muffin a good home," Rosie said.

The class had just begun when there was a message for Rosie to call home. Alarmed, she hurried from the meeting room to the Parks Department office. Her parents would not call her out of her class unless something was terribly wrong. Had there been an accident? A heart attack?

"Hello?"

"Muffin ran away." Mr. Saunders blurted out the words the second he heard Rosie's voice.

"Oh, no."

"Right after you left, I put Bone Breath outside and shut Webster in your room so Muffin could prowl around the house for a while. Muffin was in the kitchen, and your mother opened the door to carry out a bag of garbage, and when the door opened, Muffin bolted. Bone Breath saw her and chased her to the fence, and she went over it and took off. For an eleven-year-old cat, she can sure turn on the power. We've been looking for her ever since, but she's gone."

"Maybe she went back to Mrs. Tallie's house."

"That's what we thought. I went over and looked through the fence, but I didn't see her. We haven't called Mrs. Tallie yet because we hope we'll find Muffin and we don't want to upset Mrs. Tallie. We thought you might want to come home and look for Muffin. She's more likely to come to you than to us."

"I'll catch the next bus," Rosie said.

"I'll come and get you," Mr. Saunders said.

Kayo left the class, too, and went home with Rosie. When they got there, Muffin was still missing.

"Let's go to Mrs. Tallie's house," Kayo said. "Muffin might be out in the garden, in plain sight."

The gate around Mrs. Tallie's property was closed. "Do you think Mr. Cookson will mind if we search in the gardens?" Rosie said.

"Probably. But we have to find Muffin." Kayo lifted the metal handle, opened the gate, and slipped inside. Rosie followed.

"Here, Muffin," Rosie called. "Here, kitty, kitty, kitty."

They followed the path through the roses, the daylilies, and the phlox. They checked the bench where Mrs. Tallie had been sitting the day Rosie met her. Muffin was not there.

"Let's go around in back, by the herb garden," Kayo said.

The girls walked slowly, one on each side of the herb garden, searching under any plants that were large enough to shelter a cat.

"Muffin. Here, Muffin," Rosie said.

"Maybe she went in the shed," Kayo said,

pointing to a wooden shed at the back of the property. "The door is open." Kayo looked around the dim interior of the shed. Shelves held fertilizer, hand tools, a big ball of twine, and bottles of insect sprays. Kayo noted with approval that Mr. Cookson used soap sprays, rather than pesticides.

There was a push mower, with dried grass hanging like fringe from its blades. Bags of peat moss climbed one wall, and a green wheelbarrow filled with rags rested in the corner. Rakes, shovels, and hoes stood like soldiers in a row, their wooden handles ready to go into action. Muffin was not there.

While Kayo looked inside the shed, Rosie looked behind it.

When Kayo joined her, Rosie was bent over a large plant in a yellow flowerpot. "Come here," Rosie said. "Look what I found."

"What? Is she there?"

"No, but look at this plant."

Kayo looked. The plant was two feet high, with oval, toothed leaves and black berries. She didn't see anything to get excited about. "So?" she said. "What about it?"

"Do you recognize it?" Rosie asked.

Kayo shook her head.

"I think," Rosie said slowly, "this is night-shade. It's one of the poisonous plants they told us about in our Saturday class."

Kayo looked again. The plant did seem familiar.

"I'm using nightshade in my science report," Rosie said. "I drew it for one of the charts."

"Mrs. Tallie knows a lot about plants; I don't think she would grow anything poisonous."

"Maybe she doesn't know."

"If she doesn't know it is poisonous, surely Mr. Cookson does."

"I didn't mean she doesn't know it's poisonous; I meant, maybe she doesn't know the plant is here."

Something in Rosie's voice sent warning signals to every nerve in Kayo's body. She stepped away from the plant. "What are you getting at?" she said.

"Why is this plant back here, behind the shed, instead of out with all the other plants?"

"Maybe it has bugs and he's keeping it away from the other plants."

"If it had bugs," Rosie said, "he would spray and get rid of them."

"True. There are lots of different bug sprays in the shed."

Rosie's voice dropped so low that Kayo had to strain to hear her. "Everything else is planted directly in the ground," she said. "Why would Mr. Cookson leave this one plant in a flowerpot?"

Kayo removed her Mariners cap, smoothed her hair back, and replaced the cap.

Rosie answered her own question. "Because he knows it's poisonous," she said, "and he doesn't want anyone to find it. If it's in a pot, he can hide it."

The girls stood in silence for a moment, staring at the plant.

"Do you think," Kayo whispered, "Mr. Cookson tried to poison Muffin?"

"No," Rosie said. "I think he is poisoning Mrs. Tallie."

Chapter
6

"What?" Shock made Kayo's voice squeak.

"Shhh. I think Mr. Cookson is poisoning Mrs. Tallie."

"Why would he do that?" Kayo asked. "If Mrs. Tallie dies, he'll lose his job."

Rosie spoke slowly, thinking it through as she talked. "Mr. Cookson has worked for Mrs. Tallie for fifteen years, and until last month she thought she had no family. She told me herself Mr. Cookson is her best friend. Maybe she wrote a will that would leave her house and everything else she has to Mr. Cookson."

"If Mr. Cookson was in a hurry to inherit Mrs.

Tallie's property, he would have done something a long time ago."

"He wasn't in a hurry until now."

Kayo frowned, trying to keep up with Rosie's train of thought. "I think you will be a mystery writer when you grow up," she said. "You like weird words and you imagine things like poison plants and a murderous gardener."

"Now that Bert is here," Rosie continued, "Mr. Cookson knows Mrs. Tallie will change her will and leave her house and her money to Bert instead of to him."

"Why? She and Mr. Cookson have been friends for fifteen years and she just met Bert. Why would she change her will?"

"People almost always leave their property to a relative," Rosie said.

"That doesn't seem fair," Kayo said. "Still, Mrs. Tallie was thrilled to know she has a family member."

Rosie nodded. When she spoke, she was no longer tentative. "Mr. Cookson wants her to die before she gets around to changing her will, so he got a poisonous plant, hid it behind the shed, and he's putting poison in her food."

"Let's go call the police," Kayo said.

"Not yet. We need proof before we can accuse him." Because Rosie's mother was an attorney, she knew more about such matters than Kayo did.

"How are we going to get proof?"

"The first thing we need to do," Rosie said, "is learn exactly what Mrs. Tallie's symptoms are, and then we can find out the symptoms of nightshade poisoning and see if they match."

They continued around the back side of the shed and started through the herb garden, looking for Muffin in the basil and dill.

"We already know one symptom," Kayo said. "She said her stomach hurts after she eats."

"My stomach would hurt, too, if there was poison in my food."

Kayo's stomach hurt just thinking about the possibility that Mr. Cookson would poison Mrs. Tallie. They were friends; how could money, even a huge amount of money, be more important than the life of his friend?

As if she were thinking the same thing, Rosie said, "Maybe *she* thinks they're friends, but he feels differently. Maybe he got tired of her ordering him around. Maybe he wants to grow exotic orchids in the gardens, and he always has to plant zinnias and petunias because she's the boss.

38

Maybe she doesn't pay him as much as he thinks she should."

"None of those is a good reason to poison her," Kayo said.

"There is no good reason to poison someone," Rosie said. She walked faster and called Muffin with more urgency. "Here, Muffin. Come, kitty, kitty."

A voice behind them snapped, "What are you doing here?"

Startled, the girls looked around.

Mr. Cookson stood on the bottom step of the back porch, scowling at them. "If we wanted children to come in the garden, we would not have a fence around the property."

"We're looking for Muffin," Rosie explained. "She ran away and we thought she might come back here."

"We didn't call to ask permission because we didn't want to upset Mrs. Tallie," Kayo added.

"I have not seen the cat," Mr. Cookson said, "and I've been in the garden since early this morning." He moved closer. "Mrs. Tallie," he said, "does not allow anyone except me to be on her property without permission. Especially children, who always pick the flowers and trample the seedlings."

"We didn't pick any flowers," Kayo said, spreading her empty hands for him to see.

"We didn't step on the plants, either," said Rosie. "We only looked for Muffin."

"We'd like to talk to Mrs. Tallie for a moment, please," Kayo said.

"She isn't feeling well."

"I know. That's why we . . . I mean, we need to ask her for a picture of Muffin."

"That's right," Rosie said. "We want to make Lost Cat posters."

"Mrs. Tallie is much too sick to see you now," Mr. Cookson said. He didn't suggest that they try later.

"Muffin doesn't seem to be here," Kayo said, "so we'll leave now."

Mr. Cookson nodded, as if to say, *See that you do.*

"If you see Muffin," Rosie said, "will you please call us?"

"I'll watch for the cat," Mr. Cookson said. He stepped off the porch and walked toward the gate, escorting the girls out of the garden. "In the future," he said, "don't open the gate without permission."

He closed the gate behind them, making sure

it was latched, and then turned away without saying goodbye.

"What a crab," Kayo whispered as they walked away.

"Even if Mr. Cookson saw Muffin," Rosie said, "he probably wouldn't call us. He'd chase her out into the street."

"We weren't hurting anything," Kayo said, "and we did have a reason for being there. Just because they've had trouble in the past with kids coming in and picking flowers is no reason to grump at us."

"That was only an excuse. He doesn't want us or anyone else in the garden because he is afraid we'll find the nightshade."

"If he thinks we saw it," Kayo said, "maybe he'll get rid of it. Or at least hide it better."

Rosie stopped walking. "If Mr. Cookson is worried that we saw the plant, he might hide it somewhere else right now. Let's go around to the back side of Mrs. Tallie's property and peek through the fence. If we see him move the plant, it will be proof that he's guilty."

"Plus, we'd know where to find the plant when we come back with the police."

Kayo turned around and jogged back the way

they had just come. Rosie trotted after her. They passed the gate, turned the corner, and ran beside the fence that extended along the side of Mrs. Tallie's property.

When they came to a narrow alley that went between the back side of Mrs. Tallie's property and the neighboring lots, the girls ran down the alley.

By the time they reached the area where they thought the shed was, Rosie was out of breath.

Thick shrubs and trees grew all along the fence.

"I can't even see the roof of the shed," Rosie said. "There's no way to watch Mr. Cookson from here."

"Muffin could hide in there for years," Kayo said, "and we'd never find her."

"She'll come out of hiding when she gets hungry."

The girls started for home. As they passed Mrs. Tallie's gate, they saw Bert outside, picking some roses.

"Maybe we should tell Bert our suspicions," Kayo said. "He could make sure Mr. Cookson doesn't put anything in Mrs. Tallie's food."

Rosie thought a moment and then agreed. "If Mr. Cookson is innocent, we'll apologize later. But if he's guilty, Bert might be able to save Mrs. Tallie's life."

Hurrying toward the gate, the girls called, "Hi, Bert."

Bert came to greet them. "How's Muffin?" he asked.

"She ran away," Kayo said. "We're looking for her."

"I'll hunt for her here in the garden," Bert said. "Poor old Muffin. I feel terrible that my allergies caused all this trouble."

"You can't help being allergic," Kayo said.

"No," Bert agreed. "And with Aunt Hilda so sick, it's good that I'm here. She wouldn't be able to manage alone. She can't walk without help now."

Kayo and Rosie looked at each other, wondering how to say what they were both thinking.

Rosie spoke first. "There's an odd plant out behind the shed," she said, "in a big yellow pot. It has black berries on it and the leaves are oval with jagged edges. Do you know what it is?"

Bert nodded. "It's a belladonna. I bought it for

Aunt Hilda because she likes unusual flowers. Belladonna flowers are shaped like bells."

Belladonna. Rosie probed her memory. She was good at recalling names and words, and belladonna did seem familiar. Perhaps she was mistaken about the plant. Maybe she didn't recognize it from the class; maybe she had read about it in a book, or one of her dad's garden magazines.

"The belladonna is native to southern Europe and parts of Asia," Bert said. "I don't know if it will grow here, but I thought Aunt Hilda would enjoy trying it, and Mr. Cookson has a talent for making plants thrive." He frowned. "I didn't know it was still in the pot. I'll speak to Mr. Cookson about planting it. It needs this good garden soil."

Bert smiled warmly at the girls. "As soon as I put these roses in water," he said, "I'll look for Muffin. It would be best if you don't come back here to search. Aunt Hilda would be terribly upset if she knew Muffin was lost, and since there's nothing she can do about it, I don't plan to tell her."

"We won't need to search in the garden as long as you're looking here," Kayo said.

"If I see her," Bert said, "I'll have to call you to come and get her. I can't pick her up. How do I reach you?"

Rosie took her vocabulary notebook and pencil from her pocket. She wrote her phone number on a blank page, tore the page out, and gave it to Bert.

He tucked the paper in his shirt pocket. "Be sure to let me know if you find her," he said.

"We will."

The girls waved goodbye. "He's such a nice man," Rosie said. "I'm glad Mrs. Tallie has him to take care of her, even if he *is* the reason Muffin had to leave."

"You handled that perfectly," Kayo said. "We didn't even have to mention Mr. Cookson and our suspicions."

"It's a relief to know the plant isn't poisonous."

"It sure is. For a while I thought Care Club was going to be involved with an attempted murder."

"Mr. Cookson is a grouch," Rosie said, "but he isn't completely unscrupulous." She took out her vocabulary notebook and made a check.

"Unscrupulous," Kayo said, trying to remember the definition.

"Without any conscience," Rosie said. "No moral integrity."

"A crook," said Kayo.

"If you would *use* the vocabulary words," Rosie said, "it would be easy to remember them."

"In 1904 unscrupulous baseball players lost the World Series on purpose in order to win money by betting against themselves."

"Are you making that up?" Rosie said.

"It really happened. Players on the Chicago White Socks team were convicted. Afterward, everyone called them the Black Socks."

"Too bad you can't write your science report on baseball history," Rosie said. "You'd fill up six pages in no time."

The girls walked back to Rosie's house, calling Muffin.

"I hate to think of Muffin left out all night," Rosie said. "She's been a pampered pet all her life; she must be scared and hungry."

"I have to go home," Kayo said, "but I'll come back first thing tomorrow morning."

After dinner Rosie got out her science report.

Don't Go Near Mrs. Tallie

She reread the information about poisonous plants and studied the pictures. Then she went to the telephone and called Kayo.

"It's true that the plant we found is a belladonna," she said. "The other name for it is nightshade. Deadly nightshade."

"Is it poisonous?" Kayo said.

"Very."

Chapter 7

*T*hat night Rosie got the threatening phone call.

"Don't go near Mrs. Tallie. . . . Stay away—or suffer."

The words repeated in her brain like a tape playing over and over. Who called her? No one knew about her suspicions except Kayo. How could anyone know? Rosie and Kayo had only begun to feel suspicious themselves that afternoon.

My hunch must be right, Rosie thought. Mr. Cookson *is* poisoning Mrs. Tallie, and he's afraid if we keep going over there, we'll find out. So he's trying to scare us away.

She closed her eyes, remembering the voice.

Don't Go Near Mrs. Tallie

Had it been Mr. Cookson? She wasn't sure. It had not sounded like him, but the caller was probably trying to disguise his voice.

Who else knew they were helping Mrs. Tallie with Muffin? Bert did, but he had encouraged the girls to help; Bert certainly wouldn't make a threatening phone call.

People in their Saturday class at the Parks Department knew. Sammy knew. Kids at school knew. Now that she thought about it, lots of people knew that she and Kayo were trying to find a new home for Mrs. Tallie's cat. But why would any of those people want them to stop? Mr. Cookson was the only person who didn't want Rosie and Kayo near Mrs. Tallie's house.

Rosie called Kayo and told her about the phone call.

"It must have been Mr. Cookson," Kayo agreed. "Lots of people know about Care Club's Muffin project, but he is the only one who doesn't like it when we go over there."

"I feel so creepy," Rosie said. "I never got a phone call like that before."

"It makes me feel creepy, too," Kayo said. "I didn't hear the voice, but he threatened me." She took off her Toronto Blue Jays cap and twirled it

49

nervously on one finger. "What did your parents say?"

"I haven't told them yet. They're at their dance club. If I tell them, they won't let me look for Muffin anymore."

"We have to keep looking! If we don't help Muffin, who will? Mrs. Tallie is too sick and Bert's allergic."

"I want to help Muffin. But that voice on the phone was horrible."

"It makes me furious. Mr. Cookson has no right to frighten you like this."

Hearing Kayo's anger calmed Rosie and restored her courage. "I'm not going to let him scare me away," she said.

"Good. Finding a home for Muffin is an official Care Club project. I don't want to give up."

"Neither do I. But I don't want any more phone calls like that one."

"If you're sure the plant is nightshade, we should tell our parents and they can tell the police. Maybe it's against the law to have a poisonous plant and they'll take it away."

"We need evidence before we accuse him. Without evidence the police might not believe us."

"Your parents will believe you got that phone call."

"Yes, they will. And as soon as they know about it, they'll forbid me to go to Mrs. Tallie's house. How can we get proof unless we go back?"

"What do you want to do?"

"Go to Mrs. Tallie's garden and get a piece of the plant so we have proof that it was really there, even if Mr. Cookson denies it or gets rid of it. Then we'll visit Mrs. Tallie and ask her exactly what her symptoms are. We can go to the library and find out the symptoms of nightshade poisoning, and if it all matches, we'll tell the police."

"What if Mr. Cookson sees us over there?" Kayo said. "We have to go clear across the whole property to the shed where the plant is. He's sure to spot us."

"We'll say we are looking for Muffin, which will be true. What can he do except chase us away?"

"He could . . ." Kayo hesitated, not wanting to say what she was thinking.

"What?"

"He could make us suffer. Like he said on the telephone."

Rosie shuddered at the words. "People who

make anonymous, threatening telephone calls are cowards," she said. "Mr. Cookson is afraid to confront us in person."

"I hope you're right," Kayo said, "but I don't want to find out. Let's get up really early tomorrow morning. We can sneak into the garden, take a piece of the nightshade, and leave again before Mr. Cookson arrives."

"What time does it get light?"

"About six o'clock," Kayo said. "Mom gets up at six, and when I hear her, it's just starting to get light."

"Can you get over to my house that early tomorrow?"

"I'll set my alarm for five-thirty and meet you at the corner at six."

"Be careful," Rosie said.

"You, too."

Early the next morning Rosie tiptoed across the kitchen.

"Shhh," she whispered as Bone Breath wagged toward her, his toenails clicking on the tile floor. She turned on the back porch light and stepped outside, hoping Muffin might have returned during the night.

Don't Go Near Mrs. Tallie

Seeing no sign of the missing cat, she let Bone Breath out and waited while he relieved himself. If she left without doing that, Bone Breath would whine until he woke her parents.

She was glad it was Sunday. Her parents usually slept late on the morning after their dance club.

As soon as Bone Breath finished, Rosie put him inside, locked the door, and left. Slashes of pink streaked across the eastern sky, giving a reddish tinge to Rosie's house. She was too nervous to appreciate the sunrise color. Last night she had wanted to sneak into Mrs. Tallie's garden. Now she wasn't so sure.

Kayo was waiting at the corner. She wore her Field of Dreams sweatshirt, which, Rosie knew, was Kayo's lucky shirt. Her San Francisco Giants cap was jammed backward on her head, the way she wore her cap in a baseball game when she desperately needed to throw a strike.

"I thought for sure Mom would hear me get up," Kayo said, "but she didn't. I left her a note, in case she wakes up before we get back. I said we were going out to look for Muffin."

"I left a note, too."

"As long as I'm home and ready for church by

ten o'clock, Mom won't care. Her choir is singing a special anthem this morning."

"Maybe Mr. Cookson doesn't work on Sundays," Rosie said.

Encouraged by that thought, the girls hurried toward Mrs. Tallie's house.

"What will we do if the nightshade isn't where it was yesterday?" Kayo said. "If Mr. Cookson made that phone call, he must know we're suspicious, so he may already have hidden the plant."

"Or gotten rid of it," Rosie said. "If it isn't still behind the shed, I guess we'll have to search for it." She walked a bit slower. "I kept thinking about it last night, and I decided Bert must have told Mr. Cookson that we saw the belladonna."

"Bert said he was going to ask Mr. Cookson to plant it."

"Right. Bert told him we had asked about the plant and Mr. Cookson panicked. If he was already nervous that someone would find out what he was doing, the last thing he would want is for us to be able to describe the plant."

Kayo stopped walking. "Are you sure we ought to be going back there?" she said. "If Mr. Cookson is poisoning Mrs. Tallie, and if he made that awful phone call, hard telling what he will do if he catches us in the garden again. He told us yesterday not to come back."

"I'm nervous," Rosie admitted. "But if we get proof that Mr. Cookson is hiding a poisonous plant, we might save Mrs. Tallie's life."

They reached Mrs. Tallie's property and walked along the front side to the gate. They stopped at the gate, peering through the iron bars. With no breeze the garden seemed hushed, as if the flowers waited sleepily for the sun to awaken them. The windows of the house were dark rectangles against the gray walls.

"I don't think Mrs. Tallie and Bert are up yet," Kayo whispered.

"It isn't Mrs. Tallie and Bert I'm worried about," Rosie replied.

"Mr. Cookson wouldn't come to work this early," Kayo said.

"I hope not."

Rosie lifted the latch and pushed the gate open. "Care Club to the rescue," she said, and the girls stepped into the garden, closing the gate behind them.

"How did we go from helping homeless animals to preventing a murder?" Kayo said.

Instead of following the path toward the house,

as they had always done before, they walked around the edges of flower beds, staying as close to the fence and as far from the house as possible. Morning dew dampened the legs of their jeans as they brushed against tall shrubs and blooming lilies.

The pink clouds faded to white as the sun climbed. Kayo and Rosie stopped when they reached the shed. They glanced back toward the house. All was quiet.

"I wonder if Mr. Cookson uses the front gate when he comes to work," Rosie said, "or if there's a back gate somewhere."

Kayo's heart beat faster. She didn't want to think about Mr. Cookson appearing suddenly beside them through an unseen rear gate.

"There has to be a back entrance for garbage pickup and meter readers," Rosie continued. "That's why there's an alley, so service trucks can get in."

"I didn't see any back gate when we were in the alley," Kayo said.

"We probably didn't go far enough."

"Let's find the poison plant and get out of here," Kayo said.

They crept around the side of the shed, listening for any sound. When they reached the spot where they had seen the deadly nightshade, they stopped.

The plant was not there.

The girls stared at the round patch of grass, flattened and yellowed, where the pot had rested.

"He hid it," Kayo said. "That proves he's guilty."

"Maybe not. Bert told him to plant it; maybe he did."

"Then why would he call and threaten us?"

"We don't know for sure that it was Mr. Cookson," Rosie said. "He is innocent until we can prove he's guilty."

Sometimes Kayo wished Rosie didn't know so much about the law. She didn't want to have to prove anything; she just wanted to get out of Mrs. Tallie's yard before Mr. Cookson found them.

"Let's walk through the vegetable garden," Rosie said. "Maybe he put it by the green beans or the broccoli."

Kayo looked toward the plot of vegetables. The sun was higher, warm on her face. "Maybe we should forget about it and go home. Mr. Cookson might get here any minute."

"It won't take long to check out the vegetable garden."

"Remember the phone call?"

Rosie shivered, despite the warm sun. Of course she remembered the phone call. How could she forget it? Every word had replayed in her mind a dozen times. Kayo was right; they should leave before something terrible happened.

"On the other hand," Kayo said, "if Mrs. Tallie is in danger, we have to help her."

They glanced across the rows of ankle-high sweet corn. They walked past the young tomato plants and searched through the rows of beans, broccoli, lettuce, and zucchini. Except for the green pea branches twining thickly together on a wire fence, the young vegetables were too small to conceal the nightshade. The suspicious plant was not in the vegetable garden.

It was not in any of the flower beds, either.

"Let's try the herb garden," Kayo said.

Cautiously the girls moved toward the herb garden, which was near the back door of Mrs. Tallie's house. They found mint, rosemary, parsley, and chives. They did not find the nightshade.

"We should have taken a leaf when we first saw it behind the shed," Kayo said.

Don't Go Near Mrs. Tallie

"Maybe Mr. Cookson kept enough nightshade to finish the job and threw away the plant, pot and all."

They looked toward the house. A metal garbage can and three recycling containers stood on a small wooden platform just around the corner of the house from the back door.

"Let's look in the garbage can," Rosie said.

"And then let's go home."

Rosie lifted the lid off the garbage can and set it on the ground.

The girls peered inside. They saw a discarded lamp, a brown paper bag full of used Kleenex, two empty yogurt cartons, and other household trash. No plant. No yellow pot.

Someone coughed.

Rosie and Kayo stood still as stones.

The cough came again. Someone was in the garden, on the front side of the house.

Rosie put her finger to her lips. Neither girl spoke.

Without replacing the lid, both girls squatted beside the garbage can, using it to shield them from the sight of anyone who came around the corner.

They huddled together, listening.

Footsteps crunched on the gravel path that led around the side of the house.

Three black crows, who had been swaggering about on the grass between the house and the herb garden, cawed their displeasure and flapped noisily away.

"Someone's coming," Rosie whispered.

Chapter

Was it Mr. Cookson? Had he seen them? Should they stay where they were or should they run for it? The questions whirled through Rosie's mind like a spinning top. She could tell by the expression on Kayo's face that Kayo was wondering the same things.

Uncertainty and fear kept the girls from moving.

Seconds later they let out their breath in relief as they saw who it was.

"It's Bert," Kayo said.

"Thank goodness," Rosie said.

The girls stood up.

Bert hurried toward them. "What are you

doing?" he asked. "Surely you can't expect to find Muffin in the garbage can."

"We aren't looking for Muffin," Kayo said. "That is, we are looking for Muffin but not in the garbage can. We're looking for the plant you gave Mrs. Tallie."

"The belladonna? Why would you be rummaging in our garbage can for that?"

"The plant isn't where it was yesterday, and we thought maybe Mr. Cookson threw it away."

Bert's eyes narrowed. "Why are you so interested in that belladonna? And how do you know it isn't where you saw it yesterday?"

"It's poisonous," Rosie said. "You didn't know when you bought it, but belladonna has another name. It's also called nightshade."

"*Deadly* nightshade," Kayo interrupted.

"Right," said Rosie. "We think Mr. Cookson is putting poison in Mrs. Tallie's food and that's why she's sick."

Kayo added, "We want to pick a branch of the plant so we can use it as proof."

Shock flooded Bert's face. "That's ridiculous," he said. "And it's a serious charge to make against Mr. Cookson."

"Yesterday the plant was out behind the shed, in a pot," Rosie said. "Now it's gone."

"I asked him to plant it in the garden," Bert said. "No doubt he did."

"Where?" asked Kayo.

"I don't know where he planted it. He'll be here soon; I'll ask him then."

"He didn't plant it," Kayo said. "We've searched everywhere—in the flowers, in the herb garden, and in the vegetable garden. The nightshade isn't here."

Bert's dark eyes flashed angrily. "Mr. Cookson said you had agreed not to come here without permission," he said, "and now I find you've been prowling the grounds and going through our trash." He stopped, as if trying to control his anger. "Have you told anyone about your suspicions?" he asked.

"Not yet," Rosie said. "We wanted to get some proof before we told the police."

"What about your parents?"

"No," Kayo said. "No one knows. But Mr. Cookson must realize we're suspicious, because Rosie got a phone call, warning us to stay away. Who else would do that?"

"Did your parents tell the police about the phone call?"

"They don't know about it," Rosie said. "We didn't tell anyone."

Bert was quiet for a moment, as if trying to sort out all that they had told him. "If you are right about the poison," he said, "it's important to find the plant." He glanced around. "Have you looked in the shed?"

The girls shook their heads, no.

"Maybe Mr. Cookson put the plant in there."

"Let's look now," Kayo said.

"If it *is* poisonous, as you claim," Bert said, "I'll throw it out. But the idea that Mr. Cookson would harm Aunt Hilda is crazy. The phone call was probably one of your friends, trying to scare you."

"Some friend," Kayo muttered.

"Do you think the wallydraigle would do anything like that?" Rosie asked.

Kayo shook her head. "He isn't too bright," she said, "but he isn't mean. What would be the point?"

Bert strode toward the shed, with the girls scurrying beside him. For the first time since they had come through Mrs. Tallie's gate that morning, Kayo and Rosie felt calm. Now that Bert knew their suspicions, he would take charge.

Don't Go Near Mrs. Tallie

Whether or not the plant was in the shed, Bert would deal with Mr. Cookson. Best of all, he would make sure no poison got put in Mrs. Tallie's food.

The shed door was partway open. Bert pulled it open the rest of the way and held it while Rosie and Kayo stepped inside. He followed them, closing the door behind him.

Rosie glanced quickly around inside of the shed.

"I don't see the plant in here, either," Rosie said. "What do you think we should do next, Bert?"

The question froze on her lips when she turned to Bert. He had picked up a heavy pair of pruning shears, the kind Rosie's dad used to trim the lilacs. He approached Kayo from behind, his arm raised, ready to strike her on the head with them.

"Watch out!" Rosie yelled.

Bert's hand plunged forward.

Kayo turned and ducked. The pruning shears whizzed past her head.

Horrified, Kayo backed away from Bert. She reached Rosie and clutched Rosie's hand.

The girls stood together in the dim light, facing

Bert. He kept his back to the door, blocking their exit.

"I told you not to come back here," he said. "I warned you that you would suffer if you came again."

"*You* made that phone call?" Rosie said.

"For the first time in my life," Bert said, "I have a chance to be rich. I'm not going to let a couple of snoopy kids stand in my way."

Kayo looked around the shed for a possible weapon. To her left, she saw the row of shovels and rakes. *I could swing one of those like a baseball bat,* she thought. She inched sideways toward them.

"Stay where you are," Bert said.

Kayo stopped.

"What are you going to do?" Rosie asked.

"I'm going to plant petunias." He nodded toward two flat boxes of pink and white petunias on the counter.

The girls glanced at each other. Petunias? What did petunias have to do with anything? Was Bert some kind of a mental case?

"The flower bed will be six feet deep and four feet wide," Bert said. "Exactly big enough to hold two bodies. I'll plant the petunias on top." He stepped closer. "You'll make good fertilizer," he said, "and no one will ever suspect."

"Our parents know where we are," Rosie said. "They'll call the police and this garden will be swarming with cops. Do you think for one minute they won't check out a freshly dug flower bed?"

"The whole estate is freshly dug," Bert said. "Haven't you noticed? Mr. Cookson keeps all the soil worked up."

It was true. There were acres of newly dug flower beds, and the vegetable garden had recently been tilled. A fresh plot of petunias would seem perfectly natural here.

Fear seeped into the girls like water on sand, filling them with terror.

Bert reached for Kayo.

"You first," he said.

*T*here was no escape.

Kayo moved away from him, but the shed was small, and Bert stayed between the girls and the door.

There are two of us, Rosie thought. Bert is a little man and Kayo is strong. Maybe we can overpower him. She glanced quickly around the shed. She could grab one of the bug sprays and spray it in Bert's face. Or whack him with a hoe.

Bert raised the pruning shears again. He stepped toward Kayo.

Kayo screamed.

From the corner of her eye Rosie saw movement behind Bert. Something had moved inside the wheelbarrow, over in the corner. Rosie squinted at the wheelbarrow.

Muffin!

Muffin was curled on a pile of rags, watching them. Her head stuck up over the top of the wheelbarrow, and although her body lay completely still, her tail flopped nervously up and down.

As soon as Rosie saw the cat, she knew she had found the perfect weapon.

Her mind raced. She had to get to Muffin before Bert saw the cat, and she had to let Kayo know what she planned to do so Kayo could be ready to help.

Before Rosie could think of a plan, Bert swung the shears toward Kayo's head. Kayo screamed again and dropped to the floor.

"Tackle him!" Rosie cried. She bolted toward the wheelbarrow. She scooped Muffin into her arms. The startled cat struggled to get free, but Rosie held fast.

Kayo lunged forward, grabbed Bert's ankles, and yanked. He lost his balance, stumbling sideways. Kayo jerked on his ankles again, and this time his feet went out from under him. He fell backward, landing with a thud. The blow to his head stunned him, and he lay still for a moment, eyes closed.

The second Bert's head hit the floor, Rosie dropped to her knees beside him and held Muffin on Bert's face. Muffin struggled and tried to get away.

Kayo quickly sat on Bert's legs, to keep him from getting up again.

Bert dropped the pruning shears. Kayo leaned forward and knocked them across the floor.

When Bert regained his senses, he shoved Rosie and Muffin with both hands.

Muffin yowled in protest. It took every bit of strength Rosie had to keep the cat from squirming out of her grasp and running off. She fell forward across Bert's head, squashing Muffin between her chest and Bert's face.

With one hand she held on to Muffin's collar; with the other, she grabbed Bert's right hand and pushed, keeping it away from her.

Bert clawed at Rosie's back with his other hand, but she clenched her teeth and stayed where she was.

Kayo stood up, reached over to the countertop, and grabbed a ball of sturdy twine. As soon as she got off his legs, Bert kicked and twisted.

Don't Go Near Mrs. Tallie

Kayo grabbed one of his ankles and pushed as hard as she could, forcing his leg down far enough that she could kneel on it, this time facing Bert's feet. Then she grabbed his other leg and pulled it down, too.

Working quickly, she wound the twine around and around his ankles, binding them together. *My weight training paid off,* she thought as her muscles strained to keep his feet together. She tied three knots, pulling each one so tight the coarse twine burned the palms of her hands.

Bert continued to kick, even with his ankles tied together. Sitting on his legs, Kayo felt as if she were riding a bucking bronco in a rodeo.

Muffin's head squeezed out from under Rosie, followed by her front paws. Rosie had to let go of Bert's hand in order to keep Muffin from escaping.

As soon as Rosie dropped his hand, Bert reached for her head and grabbed a handful of hair. He tugged, trying to force Rosie to get up. The pain brought tears to Rosie's eyes. She thought he was going to pull her hair right out of her head, but she stayed where she was, clamping Muffin tightly against Bert's face.

71

"Help!" Rosie yelled.

Kayo turned around. She grabbed Bert's right hand and pried his fingers open, forcing him to let go of Rosie's hair. Using all of her strength, she pinned Bert's wrist to the floor.

Bert's chest heaved as he gasped for air.

"Hang on!" Rosie cried.

Seconds later Bert quit struggling, and his other hand dropped limply to his side.

"Let's get out of here," Rosie said.

"He might be faking," Kayo said. "If you let Muffin go, Bert might grab you again."

"I don't want to smother him," Rosie said.

Kayo stood up and grabbed a three-pronged hoe. She held it on her shoulder like a baseball bat, ready to swing at Bert if he tried to get up.

Cautiously Rosie eased up. Muffin rocketed away. Her back feet pushed off from Bert's face, leaving deep scratches. As Rosie got to her feet, Muffin dashed into the corner and hid behind a bag of peat moss.

Bert lay still. His eyes were swollen shut, his face was puffy, and his breath came in short, labored gasps.

Kayo dropped the hoe and picked up the ball of twine. She held it taut while Rosie cut it with

72

the pruning shears. Then Rosie held Bert's hands together while Kayo bound his wrists.

"He won't go anywhere for a little while," Rosie said.

"Let's leave Muffin in here with him so he won't recover and come after us while we call for help."

"And we'll be able to find her," Rosie said.

They left the shed, closing the door tightly behind them. They knew the fastest way to call for help would be from Mrs. Tallie's house, but without hesitation, they both turned and ran toward the gate. It would take only a few minutes to run to Rosie's house, and they wanted to get off Mrs. Tallie's property as quickly as possible.

Rosie's knees felt weak and perspiration dribbled down the back of her neck.

Kayo reached the fence first. She looked back at Rosie, who was only a few feet behind her, and then turned to open the gate.

A large padlock glinted in the sun, securely holding the gate closed.

"We're locked in," Rosie said.

Chapter

10

"The gate wasn't locked earlier," Kayo said.

"Bert must have put the padlock on after we came in this morning." Rosie shuddered. "Maybe he saw us in the yard and locked the gate to be sure we couldn't get away from him."

"We'll have to use Mrs. Tallie's telephone to call for help," Kayo said.

The girls ran toward Mrs. Tallie's front door.

When they rang the doorbell, there was no answer. They pounded on the door. No response.

Rosie tried the doorknob; it turned. "It's unlocked," she said. She pushed the door open, and the girls stepped inside.

"Mrs. Tallie?" Kayo said. "Are you here?"

Don't Go Near Mrs. Tallie

The house was still. It seemed too quiet, even for early in the morning. When the girls had been there before, soft music played in the background, but now there was no music, no sound of a person moving around, no water running or kitchen clatter.

"Maybe there's a telephone in the living room," Rosie said. She walked across the tiled entry hall and turned into the living room. Kayo stayed by the door, peering through the glass to be sure Mr. Cookson wasn't coming.

The living room drapes were closed, and the air seemed stagnant. "Kayo!" Rosie gasped. "Come here!"

Mrs. Tallie lay on the sofa, her hands folded across her chest. Her eyes were closed, and her pale face seemed translucent in the dim light. Her white hair formed a halo around her still face.

Kayo rushed to Rosie's side. "Mrs. Tallie," she said. "Can you hear us?"

Mrs. Tallie remained motionless. Rosie stared at Mrs. Tallie's chest; it did not appear to move at all. She reached for one of Mrs. Tallie's hands and then drew back without touching the elderly woman. Her stomach turned somersaults.

"I think we got here too late," Rosie said.

Kayo stood beside Rosie, trying not to cry. Then she walked to the telephone and lifted the receiver.

"What are you doing in here?"

At the sound of Mr. Cookson's voice, Kayo dropped the telephone.

Mr. Cookson strode toward her, picked up the dropped receiver, and hung it up. "I should have you arrested," he said. "You have no business coming in this house uninvited."

"No one answered when we knocked," Rosie said, "and we need to use the phone."

Kayo reached for the telephone.

Mr. Cookson pushed her hand aside. "This is not a public telephone," he said. "How did you get in? I put a padlock on the gate not ten minutes ago."

Kayo and Rosie glanced at each other. It wasn't Bert who locked the gate; it was Mr. Cookson.

"We were here before that," Rosie said.

"Bert complained yesterday about children coming in the garden," Mr. Cookson continued, "and asked me to get a lock for it."

"Mrs. Tallie is awfully still," Kayo said, "and she doesn't respond when we talk to her. We need to call an ambulance."

Don't Go Near Mrs. Tallie

Mr. Cookson seemed to notice Mrs. Tallie for the first time. He frowned and took one of her hands in his.

Kayo inched toward the telephone.

"Mrs. Tallie," Mr. Cookson said as he patted her hand. "Wake up, Mrs. Tallie."

Kayo watched to see if there was any response.

"Is she . . . is she . . ." Rosie couldn't seem to ask the question.

"She is alive," Mr. Cookson said, "but she's either in a very deep sleep or she's slipped into a coma. You're right; she needs a doctor." He picked up the telephone and dialed nine one one. "We need an ambulance," he said. "At 1535 Lincoln Avenue."

Kayo tried to grab the receiver before he hung up. She shouted, "We need the police, too! Someone tried to kill us!"

But Mr. Cookson had pressed his finger on the button, breaking the connection before Kayo spoke.

Looking flabbergasted, he held the telephone away from her. "What in the name of heaven are you talking about?" he said. "Who tried to kill you?"

"Bert did," Rosie said.

77

FRIGHTMARES

The color drained from Mr. Cookson's face. He put down the phone, staggered to a chair, and sank into it. "You must be mistaken," he said. "Bert has a warped sense of humor; he was probably playing a joke, trying to frighten you."

"It was no joke," Rosie said. "He took us in the shed and shut the door. He tried to hit Kayo with the pruning shears. He said he was going to plant petunias on our grave."

"That's ridiculous. Why would Bert try to kill you?"

"Because we were looking for the deadly nightshade plant," Kayo said. "We told him we thought you were using it to poison Mrs. Tallie."

"Deadly nightshade?" Mr. Cookson's jaw dropped. "Poison?"

Kayo rushed on, her words tumbling out like water spilling over a dam. "Bert found us outside and when we told him our suspicions, he tricked us into going in the shed with him and he tried to hit me on the head with the pruning shears and then Rosie found Muffin in the wheelbarrow and I tackled Bert and we held him down and Rosie stuffed Muffin on his face until he passed out and then we tied him up and ran." Kayo paused for breath.

Don't Go Near Mrs. Tallie

Mr. Cookson stared at her, clearly horrified. A siren pierced the silence.

"We need to unlock the gate," Rosie said.

"We need to call the police," Kayo said.

Mr. Cookson fumbled in his pants pocket and then handed Kayo a key. "I'll call the police," he said. "You let the medics in."

Rosie and Kayo ran down the front path. As soon as they were out the door, Mr. Cookson stood up, but he did not go to the telephone to call the police. Instead, he went to the door and pushed the lock button so that the door would lock automatically when it was closed. A locked door might buy him a few extra minutes of time.

Leaving the door ajar, he hurried into the kitchen, went out the back door, and started across the garden.

Rosie and Kayo unlocked the gate just as a white ambulance, with red lights whirling on the four corners of its roof, screeched up to the curb.

"I'll take the medics to Mrs. Tallie," Kayo said.

"I'll wait for the police and tell them about Bert," Rosie said. She stepped to the curb, watching for a police car.

"This way," Kayo told the medics. They

rushed after her into Mrs. Tallie's house. No one bothered to close the door.

As the medics took Mrs. Tallie's blood pressure and listened to her heart, Kayo glanced around for Mr. Cookson, to give him back the key. He wasn't there. Odd, she thought. He had seemed genuinely concerned about Mrs. Tallie. Why wouldn't he stay to see what was wrong with her?

One of the medics asked, "How long has Mrs. Tallie been unresponsive?"

"I have no idea," Kayo said as she put the key in her pocket. "She's been sick for several days and getting worse each day. We found her like this, a few minutes before we called you. My friend and I think she was being poisoned. That's why we came over."

"Poisoned?" Both the medics stopped what they were doing and stared at Kayo. "By whom? What kind of poison?"

"We think Mrs. Tallie's nephew, Bert, was putting poison in her food. Her stomach hurt when she ate, and we found a poisonous plant in the garden. My friend recognized it because she's writing a science report on poisonous plants. It's called nightshade."

Don't Go Near Mrs. Tallie

"Atropa belladonna," said one of the medics as he stuck a thin strip of plastic on Mrs. Tallie's forehead. "I had a patient once when I worked at the Poison Control Center. He was taking atropine for his gallstones and accidentally took too much, and we had to pump out his stomach. Afterward, I read about atropine and found it comes from the atropa belladonna plant, also known as deadly nightshade." He removed the strip of plastic, looked at it, and said, "Temperature is ninety-seven point three."

"Let's get her to the hospital," the other medic said.

"I always remembered that case because it was the first patient I ever saw who almost died from taking too much of his own medicine."

"Happens all the time," the other medic said.

"I know that now. I didn't then."

Kayo watched as they gently lifted Mrs. Tallie to a gurney and wheeled her out the door. As he walked beside the gurney, one of the medics talked on a cellular telephone—apparently telling a doctor the situation and getting directions for treating Mrs. Tallie.

"Start her on oxygen," said the medic with the phone, and the other medic clamped a mask over

Mrs. Tallie's nose and mouth. A clear plastic hose ran from the mask to a small oxygen tank.

Kayo followed the medics out. She closed the door behind her. They had been in the house only about three minutes; Kayo marveled at their speed and efficiency.

Rosie still stood at the curb.

As the medics pushed the gurney toward the ambulance, a neighbor rushed across the street. "What's wrong?" the neighbor asked.

"We aren't sure," one of the medics replied.

"Did she have a stroke?" the neighbor asked. "Or a heart attack?"

The medics shot Kayo a warning look, and she knew they meant she should not mention any other possibilities. Such as poison.

Without answering the neighbor, the medics rolled the gurney into the back of the ambulance and shut the door.

"We're taking her to Oakwood General Hospital," one medic told Kayo.

Seconds later the ambulance drove away.

Across town Mr. Nipper stepped out of the elevator on the tenth floor and walked toward his law office. He didn't mind coming in to work on a weekend. It was peaceful with everyone else gone, and the phones were quiet, for a change.

Mr. Nipper plucked a stack of mail from his mail slot and flipped through it as he settled into his chair. Most of the letters he set aside unopened; he would deal with them tomorrow, during regular working hours. One return address made him smile, and he slit open the envelope.

Hilda Tallie was one of his favorite clients. He appreciated her feisty, independent spirit and enjoyed her wild tales of all the things she had done in her youth, none of which, Mr. Nipper knew, were true. Mrs. Tallie had married at age seventeen and settled into her life as the wife of a prominent businessman. She had never joined the circus or traveled around the world or had any of the adventures she loved to talk about.

The most charming part about the woman was that she continued to tell her tales, even when she knew that *he* knew they weren't true. He wondered why she had written him a letter instead of calling, as she usually did.

He removed the letter and began to read.

FRIGHTMARES

To: Mr. Victor Nipper
   Karp, Maven, and Nipper, Attorneys-at-Law

Dear Mr. Nipper,
Ever since I changed my will, bequeathing my home and all my possessions to my nephew, Bertram W. Tallie, he has acted strangely. He urges me to eat—in fact, he *insists* that I eat, even when I have no appetite.

My health is worsening quickly. Something is terribly wrong, and Bert does not care. When others are around, Bert is loving and solicitous. Alone, it is another matter. I suspect he is eager for the new will to be needed.

Today I mentioned two of my husband's aunts, and Bert had no idea who I was talking about. It seems odd and makes me wonder about his claim that his grandfather and my late husband were brothers who had a falling out and quit speaking to each other. (It would be unlike Frank not to tell me he had a brother; Frank and I did not keep secrets from each other.)

I now wonder if Bert really is my nephew or if he is an imposter taking advantage of a lonely old woman.

Don't Go Near Mrs. Tallie

I am writing this at midnight so that Bert doesn't know. Your offices are closed or I would have called. I fear I may not be strong enough to talk by Monday. If I have visitors, I will ask them to mail this. If not, it will be found after my death.

Please void the changes I made to my will. Put it back the way it used to be, with half the proceeds of my home and furnishings to go to purchase new books for the county library and the other half of the money to the Home for Elderly Circus Clowns. Keep the two-thousand-dollar trust fund with proceeds for the care of my beloved cat, Muffin.

I am of sound mind, though my body is failing. I write this letter willingly and without pressure.

Signed,
Hilda Tallie

Mr. Nipper read quickly. He was used to tall tales from this client, but this time he did not think she was making up a story. For one thing, she wouldn't play games with her will. For another, the handwriting was so shaky he could barely make out some of the words. This letter was clearly penned by an extremely ill person.

She should put aside her mistrust of doctors and seek medical help, Mr. Nipper thought.

The horror of Mrs. Tallie's message made Mr. Nipper's heart race. He read the letter once more, then reached for his telephone.

As the ambulance pulled away, the neighbor walked away, too. Apparently, it did not occur to her that Kayo and Rosie might have any information.

Kayo and Rosie stood on the curb, waiting for the police to arrive.

"It makes me nervous to stand around like this," Rosie said. "That twine isn't going to hold Bert forever."

"It may be a while before the police come," Kayo said. "When our apartment got robbed, the police didn't get there for almost an hour after Mom called them. They said unless someone's life is in danger, they don't always respond immediately."

"Our lives *are* in danger," Rosie said.

"Maybe Mr. Cookson didn't explain that."

"Maybe we should wait in the house," Kayo said.

Don't Go Near Mrs. Tallie

"I think we should call again," Rosie said. "When Mr. Cookson called the second time and gave the same address, the emergency operator might have assumed he was calling about Mrs. Tallie again, and since the medics were already on their way, that second call may have been ignored."

The girls hurried back up the path toward Mrs. Tallie's door. The door was locked.

They stood uncertainly on the porch. "Let's try the back door," Rosie said.

"Mr. Cookson locked us out," Kayo said. "He must have. The medics didn't lock the door, and nobody else has been in the house."

"Maybe he never called the police," Rosie said, "and now he is making sure we don't call them, either."

"Let's get out of here," Kayo said. "We can call the police from your house."

As they ran back to the gate, a green sedan drove down the street. It parked in front of Mrs. Tallie's house. Two men in dark suits got out of the car.

Rosie and Kayo hesitated. "What if Bert is part of the Mafia?" Rosie whispered. "Maybe he's called in two of his hit men to wipe us out."

Kayo's eyes grew wide. "Are you serious?" she said. She stepped backward, toward Mrs. Tallie's house. She knew the Mafia was a large group of criminals who stopped at nothing to get their own way.

"Bert is unscrupulous," Rosie said. "His friends are probably crooks, too." She made a mental note to put a check mark in her notebook later. Right now she had other things besides vocabulary words to deal with. Such as the two muscular men who had just come through Mrs. Tallie's gate.

"Is this the home of Hilda Tallie?" one of the men asked.

"Yes," said Rosie. "But she isn't here. She went to the hospital."

"Who are you?" the man asked.

The best defense is offense, Kayo thought. Aloud, she said, "Who are you?"

Both men reached in their pockets and produced photo identification. They held the ID and let Kayo and Rosie look.

Officer Bremner and Officer Schuman. Oakwood Police Department.

"You're cops?" Kayo said.

"Bert tried to kill us," Rosie said.

Don't Go Near Mrs. Tallie

"Bert who?'

"Bert Tallie. Mrs. Tallie's nephew."

Quickly Rosie and Kayo told the two officers what had happened.

Officer Bremner said, "Show us where the shed is."

"Don't let the cat out," Rosie said.

Officer Schuman rolled his eyes. "We're dealing with a possible homicide," he muttered, "and she worries about a cat."

"Muffin saved our lives," Kayo said.

Rosie and Kayo ran toward the back of the estate, leading the police officers to the shed.

As they drew near it, Rosie cried, "Kayo! The shed door is open!"

They rushed inside.

Bert was gone.

Chapter

11

Muffin was gone, too.

The two police officers glanced around the empty shed.

"I didn't think he would get loose so fast," Kayo said. "I made triple knots."

"He had help," Officer Bremner said. "Your knots are still intact; the twine's been cut."

The lengths of twine that Kayo had used to tie Bert's hands and feet lay on the floor, neatly snipped in two. The pruning shears lay beside them.

"Mr. Cookson must have freed Bert," Rosie said. "When I got back inside with the medics, Mr. Cookson was gone."

Don't Go Near Mrs. Tallie

"And no one else knew Bert was in the shed," Kayo said.

Officer Schuman asked, "Who's Mr. Cookson?"

"The gardener," Kayo said. "At first we thought he was the one who was poisoning Mrs. Tallie, but it turned out to be Bert. Or maybe it was both of them."

Officer Bremner strode out the door. "I'll start searching the grounds," he told his partner. "You get descriptions of both men and report in. The kids can wait in the car."

"Follow me," Officer Schuman said to Rosie and Kayo. He ran back to the green car, with the girls at his heels. "Get in the backseat and stay there," he said.

As Rosie and Kayo climbed in the backseat, Officer Schuman called police headquarters and reported what had happened. He asked the girls what Bert and Mr. Cookson looked like and repeated their descriptions into the telephone.

"Do you know if either of them had a vehicle?" he asked. "A car? A gardening truck?"

"I don't know," Kayo said.

"Mrs. Tallie told me that Mr. Cookson lived nearby," Rosie said, "but she didn't say if he walked to work or drove."

91

The officer concluded his call by saying, "Get permission for us to search the house. And send a car to drive these girls to headquarters." He told Kayo and Rosie to stay in the car until the other officer arrived. "Keep the doors locked," he said. "If you see Bert Tallie or Mr. Cookson, honk the horn."

He dashed back through the gate and ran up the path.

Both girls leaned toward the window, staring at Mrs. Tallie's property. Their glance swept across the rose garden, the front porch, and along the fence, watching for any sign of Bert or Mr. Cookson.

"If Mr. Cookson cut Bert loose," Rosie said, "it means they must have plotted this together. Maybe they had an agreement that no matter which of them inherited Mrs. Tallie's property, they would split the money. A house like this is worth a lot."

Kayo removed her Giants cap, wiped her brow with her forearm, and replaced the cap. "Bert and Mr. Cookson are certainly good actors," she said. "Bert acted shocked when we told him our suspicions, and Mr. Cookson seemed shocked when we told him what Bert had done."

"Bert *was* shocked when we told him our sus-picions—shocked that we figured out what was going on."

"It was bad enough when I thought Mr. Cookson made the phone call," Rosie said. "It's almost worse to know the caller was Bert. I liked Bert. I trusted him."

"So did I." Kayo sighed. "I wonder if we'll ever see Muffin again. She was so scared when I held her on Bert, she'll probably never come back."

A knock on the street-side window of the car made both girls jump and turn that way.

Sammy Hulenback sat on his bicycle, with the handlebars resting against the side of the police car. Sammy cupped his hands on both sides of his head and peered in the window.

Kayo pushed the window control, lowering the back window slightly.

"Did you get arrested?" Sammy asked.

"No," Kayo said. "Of course not."

"This is an unmarked cop car," Sammy said. "I can tell by the spotlights and the license plate."

"We're helping the police," Rosie said.

"Again?" Sammy's eyes widened with surprise. "What is it with you guys? First you caught the cat burglar, and then you found the school vandals, and now—what are you doing now?"

Under ordinary circumstances Rosie and Kayo might have tried to fool Sammy by saying something like, "We can't tell you. It's a highly secret, classified operation." But they were both too shocked by what had happened to make jokes about it.

"This street is unsafe right now," Rosie said. "You'd better leave."

Sammy glanced nervously over both shoulders. Seeing nothing unusual, he turned back to the window. "Why would the cops need help from you?" he said.

"There was an attempted murder," Kayo said, "and the suspect got away. The police are hunting for him, and we're watching for him, too."

"Are you witnesses?" Sammy asked. "Did someone try to kill the old woman who lives in this house?"

"He tried to kill me," Kayo said. Saying the words made the hair on her arms stand on end.

"I was going to be next," Rosie said.

Sammy pressed his forehead against the roof of the car and gaped through the opening at the top of the window. "Are you kidding me?"

"I wish we were," said Kayo.

"Who was it?"

Kayo glanced at Rosie, unsure if they should tell or not.

"It was an unscrupulous person," Rosie said. She would make two checks in her notebook, if she ever relaxed again.

"Why would anyone want to kill you?" Sammy said.

"It's a long story and we aren't supposed to talk about it until we've testified to the police," Rosie said.

"Wow." Sammy stared at them, clearly impressed by their brush with danger.

"You really should leave, in case he comes back," Kayo said.

"I have something to tell you," Sammy said. "Can I get in the cop car with you?"

"No!" said Kayo and Rosie together.

"You can tell us from there," said Rosie, "but make it fast."

"I can have the cat," Sammy said. "My mom said it's okay."

"Muffin is lost. She ran away," Kayo said. "Sorry." She reached for the control to close the window.

"What does she look like? I'll hunt for her."

"Brown with black stripes," Rosie said. "There's an *M* on her forehead."

"We're supposed to be watching for the suspect," Kayo said. "Goodbye." She closed the window.

Sammy looked up and down the street and then rode off, pedaling hard.

They turned their attention back to Mrs. Tallie's property.

"I thought the police would be back here by now," Kayo said. "How long does it take to search Mrs. Tallie's property?"

"Maybe they went out the back way," Rosie said, "to search in the alley."

Kayo grabbed Rosie's arm. "Look!" she cried. "There's Muffin!"

Kayo pointed.

Muffin sat just inside the fence, halfway between the gate and the corner, peeking out between the bars.

"Maybe she would let us pick her up, if we move slowly and quietly," Rosie said. She unlocked the door on her side.

"We're supposed to stay in the car," Kayo said.

They watched Muffin for a few seconds. "If we

don't catch her now," Rosie said, "we may never get another chance."

"If Bert and Mr. Cookson were still on Mrs. Tallie's property," Kayo said, "the police would have found them by now."

"If they are not on Mrs. Tallie's property," Rosie said, "they won't see us go after Muffin. Shall we risk it?"

"You can't steal second with your foot on first," Kayo said. "Let's go."

Rosie opened the door and they both got out. They looked in all directions. The street was deserted.

They hurried through the gate and headed around the flower beds toward Muffin. They were about six feet away from her when Muffin saw them.

"Good Muffin," Rosie said softly. "Nice kitty."

Muffin crouched low to the ground.

Rosie stepped closer. Muffin's tail swished nervously.

"Good Muffin," Kayo said. "Good cat." She circled around, to get on the other side of Muffin. If Muffin tried to run from Rosie, Kayo would be there to intercept her.

Rosie took another step toward Muffin. She

bent slowly forward, but before her hands reached the cat, Muffin bolted away from her. Instead of going toward Kayo, Muffin streaked past Rosie, toward the gate.

Rosie made a frantic grab as Muffin went past. She only managed to reach the last two inches of Muffin's tail, which slid instantly out of her grasp.

"Catch her!" Kayo cried. Both girls rushed after the cat.

Muffin stayed close to the fence, easily going under the branches of rosebushes that Rosie and Kayo had to go around. The girls were only halfway back to the gate when Muffin dashed through it and took off down the sidewalk. She was not accustomed to running and had a stiff-legged gait that made her back tilt up and down like a rocking horse. But despite her awkward trot, she was far faster than either of the girls.

By the time they were out the gate, Muffin was at the corner. She ran across the street without hesitation. "Lucky for her there weren't any cars coming," Rosie puffed.

In the middle of the next block a dog barked on the opposite side of the street. Muffin instantly turned right, leaving the sidewalk. She dashed along the side of a house, into the back yard.

When Kayo and Rosie were opposite the barking dog, they also turned and ran toward the back of the house. It was one of a row of old houses which had once been elegant homes, like Mrs. Tallie's, but had been converted to duplexes, triplexes, or even, in a few cases, fourplexes. This one was a duplex.

When they reached the back of the duplex, Muffin was out of sight. "We can't strike out now," Kayo said. "We almost had her."

"You go one way; I'll go the other," Rosie said. "She's old and not used to running. Maybe she'll get tired and hide somewhere, like she did in the wheelbarrow."

Kayo started to her right, past the back of the duplex, while Rosie went across the strip of lawn toward the back of the triplex next door. They moved silently, not wanting to scare Muffin if she was nearby.

As Rosie passed the triplex, she glanced at a small screened-in porch that rested between the back steps and the entry door. A patch of bright yellow caught her eye, and she looked more closely.

Then she turned and ran toward Kayo, who was parting the branches in some shrubbery along the far side of the duplex. When Kayo saw Rosie approaching, she went to meet her. "Did you find Muffin?" she asked.

"No," Rosie whispered. "But I found the nightshade."

Together, the girls sneaked back to the triplex. The nightshade stood in a corner of the screened porch, still in the same yellow pot.

"Mr. Cookson must live here," Kayo said.

"Or Bert has a friend who lives here," Rosie said. "We need to tell the police."

"What about Muffin? It isn't safe for her to be running loose; she'll get hit by a car or caught by a big dog."

"It isn't safe for us to be running around here, either," Rosie said. "Mr. Cookson and Bert could be in that building right at this moment."

Kayo scanned the triplex windows. No one appeared to be watching them. Even so, she agreed that they should return to Mrs. Tallie's house and tell the police officers what they had found. It was foolish to take a chance that Bert would see them here, especially since Muffin could be six blocks away by now.

Don't Go Near Mrs. Tallie

They hurried along the side of the triplex toward the street. The dog barked again. As the girls crossed the front lawn toward the sidewalk, the door of the closest triplex unit opened. Alarmed, both girls turned.

For one awful moment, they froze, staring straight into Bert's eyes. Then Bert took the front steps two at a time and started after them.

Chapter

12

"Run!" yelled Rosie. She sprinted down the sidewalk, with Kayo behind her.

Kayo ran as if she represented the tying run in the ninth inning. She passed Rosie, intending to get in the police car and leave the door open for her. She could start honking the horn, to summon help, and then as soon as Rosie was in the car, they would lock the doors.

She looked back over her shoulder, to see how far behind her Rosie was.

Bert thundered down the sidewalk, gaining on Rosie with every stride.

"Hurry!" Kayo shouted. "Faster!"

She saw Rosie surge ahead, like a car that's

shifted into overdrive. Kayo faced forward again and panic seized her. The police car was gone.

She looked quickly up and down the street as she ran, but the police car was not there.

No people were visible, either. It was Sunday morning in a peaceful residential area, and despite all that had happened to Rosie and Kayo already that day, it was not yet nine o'clock. The neighbor who was concerned about Mrs. Tallie earlier had returned to her home. No one else was about.

Kayo's brain moved even faster than her legs, thinking what their options were. They could knock on a stranger's door and ask for help, but what if no one answered? There wasn't time to make a mistake. If no one was home to answer the door they chose, there would not be time to try another house. She wondered where the neighbor lived who had come over earlier, when the medics were there.

Kayo got to Mrs. Tallie's gate, and as soon as she saw it, she remembered she had the key to the padlock in her pocket. Once the gate was locked, Bert could not get in.

She ran into the garden and closed the gate partway, leaving room for Rosie to get through.

She grabbed the padlock and prepared to click it together as soon as the gate shut.

Rosie, her face red from running so fast, approached the gate. Bert was a few yards behind her.

Rosie dashed through the opening. Kayo slammed the gate shut and clamped the lock in place.

Bert grabbed the metal bars and shook them. For an instant the two girls stood still, watching him. He had a savage, furious look in his eyes, like a wild animal who has no control over his own actions. "You won't get away," he growled.

The girls dashed toward the house.

"You can't escape," Bert called after them. "I'll find you." He turned away from the gate and ran back along the sidewalk.

"The other gate," Rosie panted. "He'll go around to the alley and come in that way."

"We'll call nine-one-one again," Kayo said. "The police can't be far away."

They ran to the back door, relieved to find that it was unlocked.

"I'll make the call," Rosie said as she pushed open the door. "You lock all the doors."

"Bert lives here," said Kayo. "He will have a key."

Don't Go Near Mrs. Tallie

Rosie and Kayo rushed inside.

From upstairs a man's voice called, "Who's there?"

The girls stopped, unsure whether to answer or to leave.

Rosie mouthed the words, "Mr. Cookson?"

Kayo shrugged.

Officer Bremner clumped down the stairs.

"There you are!" he said. "Where did you go?"

"We saw Muffin," Kayo said. "We tried to catch her and—"

Officer Bremner interrupted. "Schuman's out looking for you," he said. "So is the car that came to take you to headquarters. The whole Oakwood police force has been alerted that you're missing." He glared at the girls. "We told you to stay in the car with the doors locked, and the next thing we know, you've disappeared."

"We didn't think you would—" Kayo began.

"That's right," snapped Bremner. "You didn't think."

"We found the nightshade plant," Rosie said.

Curiosity replaced the anger in Officer Bremner's voice. "Where?"

Rosie described the location of the triplex. "Bert Tallie was there, too," she said.

105

"When we left, Bert saw us and chased us," Kayo said. "We ran here and closed the gate and locked him out, but he's probably going around to the back."

Officer Bremner said, "Go in the bathroom and lock the door. Stay there until I come for you. *Do you understand?*"

"Yes, sir," Rosie said.

"Here's the key for the gate," Kayo said, handing it to him.

The girls scurried into the small bathroom that adjoined the entry hall. Rosie locked the door. They could hear Officer Bremner talking on his phone, but his voice quickly faded into the distance, and they knew he had left the house.

Sirens wailed outside.

"I wish there was a window in here," Kayo said. "If they catch Bert, I want to see what happens."

Rosie plopped down on the closed toilet seat. "Not me," she said. "I don't ever want to see Bert again. I just want to go home."

Less than five minutes later they heard voices in the hall.

"Someone's coming," Kayo whispered. She

Don't Go Near Mrs. Tallie

knelt and tried to see through the small crack between the bottom of the door and the floor.

Rosie stood and gripped the sink, listening.

A tap on the bathroom door brought Kayo to her feet.

"You can come out," Officer Bremner said.

Kayo opened the door; she and Rosie stepped into the hall.

Officer Bremner and Officer Schuman were walking into the living room with Mr. Cookson between them.

"How did you get here so fast?" Mr. Cookson said. "I just called."

When the police did not answer, Mr. Cookson sank onto the sofa, rubbing his hands together nervously. "I never expected anything like this," he said. "I thought Bert had reformed. I thought my idea would make everybody happy—Mrs. Tallie, me, and Bert—and instead everything went wrong."

"Did you read him his rights?" Officer Bremner asked.

"Yes," said Officer Schuman.

"Suppose you start at the beginning, Mr. Cookson," Officer Bremner said, "and tell us about your idea."

"It came to me the day Mrs. Tallie told me she had to sell the house," Mr. Cookson said. "She didn't want to, you know. She's lived here fifty-some years and she wanted to stay, but it's too big for her. Six bedrooms. Four bathrooms. What does one person, living alone, need with all this space? Even after she closed off the third floor, the maintenance and cleaning were more than she could handle by herself."

"Your idea?" said Officer Bremner. "Tell us your idea."

"Well, I was worried sick when she told me she had to sell. She had an appraiser come, and the appraiser felt the house and acreage would bring nearly half a million."

Officer Bremner let out a low whistle.

"This area is zoned for multiple family dwellings," Mr. Cookson continued, "and a fourplex is worth a lot more money than a rose garden. I knew as soon as the place sold I'd be out of a job, and where am I going to find another one, at my age?"

Mr. Cookson shifted around on the sofa, as if he couldn't get comfortable. "It didn't seem right that Mrs. Tallie had to leave her home and I had to lose my job when neither of us wanted it to happen. And then it came to me that Bert could live with Mrs. Tallie and take care of the house for her and do her cooking besides. Bert's always liked to cook; his lemon pie won first prize in a contest once. I'll never forget it. I was so proud of Bert that day."

"You thought Bert could live with Mrs. Tallie?" prompted Officer Bremner.

"Yes. I thought this would be a good place for Bert to live. It would give him something to do, some purpose to his life, and it would help Mrs. Tallie at the same time. And I would keep my job."

He put his head in his hands briefly, then took a deep breath, looked up, and continued. "I believed Bert when he told me he had changed. He said he was applying for jobs, but it's hard to find work when you have a record, you know. Nobody wants to hire an ex-con."

The two officers glanced at each other.

"One of the terms of his parole," Mr. Cookson continued, "was for him to take an anger management class, and he hasn't missed a single session. I thought he had changed."

"What was he in for?" Officer Schuman asked.

"Assault. He served three years and got out on

parole. I thought he had learned his lesson. I wanted to help him, so I told him my idea for him to live with Mrs. Tallie, and right away he said he wanted to do it."

Something's wrong with this story, Rosie thought, but she couldn't figure it out and listen at the same time.

Mr. Cookson continued. "It was Bert's idea to pretend to be related to Mrs. Tallie. He invented a story about his grandfather being brother to Mrs. Tallie's husband, and she believed him. I never liked lying to her that way; it didn't seem right when she's been so good to me all these years. But Bert said if she knew the truth, she would be nervous to have him around, and I could see some sense to that, so I went along with him."

"He *isn't* related?" Kayo blurted.

Mr. Cookson looked at her, as if realizing for the first time that the girls were hovering in the doorway.

"Mr. Tallie never had a brother," Mr. Cookson said. "Bert made all that up. But he did it with good intentions, to make Mrs. Tallie feel easy about having him there with her."

Officer Bremner's beeper went off. He made a

quick call and then said, "Mrs. Tallie's blood showed a dangerous level of atropine. It seems you girls were right. Someone was poisoning her."

"Oh, no," Mr. Cookson groaned. "It was Bert, wasn't it?"

"We don't know," Officer Bremner said. "Please continue."

"Bert pretended his name was Bert Tallie," Mr. Cookson said. "He wrote Mrs. Tallie a letter saying his grandfather and her late husband were brothers who had a disagreement in their teens and never spoke to each other again. He asked if he could visit her. A week later he moved in and everything went fine except that Bert was allergic to Mrs. Tallie's cat. Then Mrs. Tallie got sick and . . ."

He suddenly stopped talking and his eyes filled with tears. "Why would Bert do that?" he said. "Why would he poison that good woman?"

"Where is Bert now?" Officer Schuman asked.

"Gone. After I cut him loose, I took him home with me. It was a while before he could open his eyes more than a slit. I gave him some antihistamine and told him to lie down and rest until he felt better, but he was too jumpy. He kept walking around, and then he looked out the window, and when he saw those girls going around the side of our building, he—he snapped."

Mr. Cookson stood up and paced around the room. "Bert's temper is his big problem, you know. It's gotten him in trouble for years. Even when he was a little boy, he sometimes blew up over nothing."

"You said he's gone," Officer Bremner said. "Gone where?"

"I don't know. When he saw those kids, he dashed out of the house after them, and five minutes later he ran back in, took the keys to my car, and left."

"What kind of car?" Officer Bremner asked.

"Ford."

"Color?"

"White."

"License number?"

Mr. Cookson gave it. Officer Schuman immediately made a call.

"There's one thing you haven't explained," Officer Bremner said. "After these girls told you

Don't Go Near Mrs. Tallie

Bert tried to kill them, why did you set him free?
Why would you take him home and try to help
him?"

Mr. Cookson stopped pacing and looked out
the window at the flowers.

"You must have realized he *wasn't* reformed," Officer Bremner said, "so why let him
get away?"

"I couldn't stand to think of him in prison
again," Mr. Cookson said. "It was terrible. Terrible!" He pounded his fist on the window
ledge. "I saw him in court wearing handcuffs
and ankle chains. Chains, mind you, like a wild
animal. I don't think I can go through it again."

"The courts decide who goes to prison," Officer Bremner said. "Not you."

Mr. Cookson turned to face Officer Bremner.
"Do you have any children?" he asked.

Officer Bremner nodded. "A little girl. Jessica."

"Then maybe you can imagine what it's like
to see your child locked up—to have him behind
bars when you go to visit."

"Bert is your son?" Officer Bremner said.

"My only child."

Kayo looked at Rosie and saw her own shock
reflected in Rosie's eyes.

113

"I had such hopes for him," Mr. Cookson said. "I don't know what went wrong."

"What is Bert's full name?" Officer Bremner asked.

"Bertram Roy Cookson." Mr. Cookson's voice broke and he hung his head as he added, "He was named after my father."

Chapter

I got in major-league trouble," Kayo said.

"So did I," said Rosie.

The girls were at Rosie's house, late Monday afternoon. As soon as Mrs. Saunders got home, she was going to go with them to visit Mrs. Tallie.

"No allowance for a month," said Kayo.

"Ouch. I lost TV privileges, and I have to take Mom's turn to do the dishes all week."

While they talked, Rosie cut a flea collar into six pieces. She put two pieces in Bone Breath's bed, two in Webster's bed, tucked one under a sofa cushion, and stuck the last one in the vacuum cleaner bag.

"Mom wasn't angry that I left the house so early," Kayo said, "since I did leave a note. But she blew her top when she heard we got out of the police car to chase Muffin, after Officer Schuman told us to stay in the car."

Rosie nodded. "My parents didn't like that, either. But they didn't yell at me until they found out about the phone call. Then they went into orbit. They said I absolutely, positively should have told them about the phone call. And you know something? They're right. I should have told them."

"Care Club struck out that time," Kayo agreed. "Mom says it's good to be independent, but we have to use some sense. As soon as we suspected Mrs. Tallie was being poisoned, we should have told an adult." She sat on the floor and put her head to her knees, stretching her leg muscles.

"My dad said if anything or anyone ever scares me again, he wants to know about it. Period. He says there are a lot of unscrupulous people in the world, and we have to be careful." She took out her notebook and made a check beside *unscrupulous*.

"Did your dad really say *unscrupulous*, or are you just using your vocabulary word?"

Don't Go Near Mrs. Tallie

"He said mean people," Rosie admitted. "He also said he's proud of us for helping Mrs. Tallie."

"I'm glad she's all right."

"Mom told me she has a wonderful surprise for Mrs. Tallie," Rosie said, "but she didn't say what it is."

"The best surprise would be if we found Muffin."

"Let's make Lost Cat posters and put them on telephone poles," Kayo said.

"And we could put a lost ad in the newspaper," Rosie said.

"Care Club doesn't have any money to pay for an ad."

"My parents would probably pay for it. It could be Mom's U.K. for today." Mrs. Saunders tried to do one unexpected kindness every day, and Rosie was often surprised by what her mother chose to do. Usually, it was something simple, like letting a person with only one or two items go in front of her in the checkout line, but occasionally her unexpected kindness (Mr. Saunders and Rosie called it her U.K.) was something that the recipient couldn't afford. Once she bought hearing aids for a woman she'd never met. Another time she gave opera tickets to the garbage collector.

The telephone rang. When Rosie answered, Sammy Hulenback said, "Hi, Rosie. Is Kayo at your house?"

"No," said Rosie. "She got a job at Disney World and moved to Florida."

"This is important," said Sammy.

"Just a minute," Rosie said. She covered the mouthpiece with her hand and whispered, "It's your admirer."

"Tell him I just left. Tell him I was a first-round draft choice for the New York Yankees."

"He says it's important," Rosie said, handing the phone to Kayo.

Kayo said, "Hello."

"Come over to my house right away," Sammy said.

"I can't," Kayo said. "We're going to go visit Mrs. Tallie. She got out of the hospital this afternoon." *Not that I would go to his house anyway,* Kayo added silently. The last time he asked her to come over, he had wanted her to see a dead squirrel.

"Can't you come here first?" Sammy asked. "I have something to show you."

"Rosie's mother is going with us. What do you want to show me?"

Don't Go Near Mrs. Tallie

"I found the cat," Sammy said.

"You found Muffin?" Kayo said. "Are you sure it's her?"

"She has an *M* on her forehead," Sammy said. "Where was she?"

"I was riding my bike by that big old house where you were in the police car, and there was the cat, sitting on the sidewalk by the front gate."

"And she let you pick her up?" Kayo could hardly believe it.

"I went home and got a big cardboard box and put some tuna in it and set it down a few feet away from her. The cat took one sniff of that tuna and jumped into the box. I just shut the flaps and carried her home. I can't decide what to name her."

"Her name is Muffin."

"That's a sissy name. It was okay for that old woman, but I'm going to name her either Dude or Vampire."

"She does not need a new name," Kayo said. "And she doesn't need a home anymore, either. Mrs. Tallie's nephew is gone, so Mrs. Tallie can keep Muffin."

Rosie said, "Tell him we'll pick Muffin up on our way to Mrs. Tallie's house. I still have Muffin's carrier."

Kayo relayed the message.

"No," Sammy said.

"Well, then, when should we come to get her?"

"Never. I'm keeping the cat. But you can come to see her whenever you want to."

"You can't keep her," Kayo said. "She belongs to Mrs. Tallie."

"You told me yourself this cat needed a home," Sammy said.

"And I also told you Muffin would be afraid of Napoleon."

"Maybe not."

"It really doesn't matter if she's scared of Napoleon or not," Kayo said, "because Muffin is Mrs. Tallie's cat, and she's going to live with Mrs. Tallie."

"The cat was lost and I found her," Sammy said.

"She wasn't lost!" Kayo said. "She was sitting in front of her own garden gate, waiting to be let in. You have to give her back."

"What's it worth to you?" Sammy said.

"You want us to *pay* to get Muffin back?" Kayo made a fist with her free hand and shook it at the telephone.

Rosie's mouth dropped open.

"No," said Sammy. "I want you to let me join your club."

"What club?"

"The one you and Rosie have. I don't know what you call it, but you're always doing exciting stuff with burglars and vandals and murderers, and I want to do it, too."

"Our club membership is full," Kayo said.

"Then I'm keeping the cat," said Sammy. "Unless . . ."

"Unless what?"

"I might consider trading the cat for your Ken Griffey Junior rookie card."

"Are you out of your mind?" cried Kayo. "I wouldn't trade that baseball card if you had a solid-gold cat with emerald eyes. Never! Never, never, never!"

"I think you'd better let me talk to him," Rosie said as she snatched the receiver away from Kayo.

Kayo stomped around the room, muttering to herself.

"You listen to me, Sammy," Rosie said. "We'll be there to pick Muffin up in half an hour, and if you don't give her to us, you'll have to deal with my mother in court!" She slammed the receiver down, without waiting for Sammy to reply.

"Can you believe it?" Kayo said. "He wants to join Care Club."

"Over my dead body," said Rosie.

"And he wants my Ken Griffey Junior rookie card!"

"Creep," said Rosie. "Creep, creep, creep."

When Mrs. Saunders got home, the girls told her about Sammy's call. Mrs. Saunders went straight to her study and closed the door. The girls could hear her talking on the telephone, but they couldn't hear what she said.

She emerged a minute later and said, "Let's go."

"What about Muffin?" Rosie asked.

"Bring the cat carrier. We're picking Muffin up before we go to Mrs. Tallie's house."

"But Sammy—" Rosie began.

"Mr. Hulenback will deal with his son."

"I hope Sammy gets grounded for a month," Kayo said, "so he won't be able to bother us."

"A year would be even better," said Rosie.

"I suggested that Sammy should write you a letter of apology," Mrs. Saunders said.

"Oh, no," said Rosie.

Don't Go Near Mrs. Tallie

"I hope he doesn't do it in poetry," Kayo said. "Remember when he wrote that disgusting love poem to me?"

"It was no worse than the get-well poem he wrote to me," said Rosie.

"I don't think I could stand to read another of Sammy's stupid poems."

When they reached Sammy's house, Mrs. Hulenback answered the door. Muffin was easily transferred from the cardboard box to her carrier. Much to Kayo's and Rosie's relief, Sammy did not appear.

"Oh!" Mrs. Tallie cried when the girls and Mrs. Saunders arrived with Muffin. "You've brought my darling home."

As soon as the carrier was opened, Muffin jumped in Mrs. Tallie's lap and began to purr loudly.

"I never thought I'd see my precious pussycat again," Mrs. Tallie said as she stroked Muffin's fur.

"How are you feeling?" Kayo asked.

"Much better, thank you. When I got the poison out of my system and some decent food in, I improved. I can't thank you girls enough. If you hadn't come . . ." She shook her head sadly. "Now that I know the truth, it's hard to admit I was so gullible. I believed Bert's story."

Rosie took out her notebook and wrote *gullible*. She would look it up when she got home.

"He was charming," Mrs. Tallie went on, "and he tried so hard to please me. I even changed my will, leaving everything to Bert. Of course, I changed it back again after I got suspicious."

"Good," said Rosie.

"I'll find an apartment that allows cats," Mrs. Tallie said. "I hate to give up my home, but it was worse to give up Muffin. It's ironic, isn't it? I own property worth half a million dollars, yet I can't afford to stay here." She shook her head. "Housekeepers are expensive," she said. "On paper, I have a lot of money, but there isn't enough each month in my checking account."

"I know the feeling," Kayo said.

"I thought nothing would be worse than having to move," Mrs. Tallie said. "When Bert came along, I was so relieved at the chance to stay here in my house, I would have believed almost anything." Mrs. Tallie sighed. "How could I have been so foolish?"

"I've found a way for you to remain here in

your house," Mrs. Saunders said. "That's why I came with the girls; I'd like to explain it to you."

"Please do." Mrs. Tallie leaned forward in her chair.

"It's called a reverse mortgage," Mrs. Saunders said. "You would sell your house to a bank now, but you could remain here for the rest of your life. Every month you would receive a payment— enough to enable you to hire household help and live comfortably. When you die, the bank takes possession and your heirs receive whatever is still owed."

"It sounds too good to be true," Mrs. Tallie said.

"I assure you it's perfectly legal," Mrs. Saunders said. "The bankers think that the house will be worth more in the future, when they finally take possession, than what they pay for it now, so they make a profit. Meanwhile, you get part of the money now, when you need it. I will be happy to arrange it for you, if you want me to."

Mrs. Tallie beamed, brushing tears of joy from her eyes. "We get to stay here," she told Muffin. "Together."

The doorbell rang; Mr. Cookson stood on the porch.

"Because I turned myself in and cooperated with the police, I'm free until the hearing," he told Mrs. Tallie. "I came to apologize. I didn't suspect that Bert was poisoning you, but I should not have let him lie about being your nephew. I should have told you who he was, right from the start."

"You never mentioned a son," Mrs. Tallie said.

"Bert has been in trouble since he was in junior high," Mr. Cookson said. "He shamed me so many times, I quit talking about him." He walked to the sofa and sat beside Mrs. Tallie.

"I thought it was a way to help everyone," Mr. Cookson said. "I would keep my job, you would stay in your house, and Bert would do something useful. I believed him when he said he had changed. I wanted to help him be a productive, good citizen, but I should not have gone along with his plan to lie about his identity. I'm sorry."

"Lying is always wrong," Mrs. Saunders said, "even when it's for a good cause."

"I apologize to you girls, too," Mr. Cookson said. "After you told me that he attacked you, I should not have helped him get away so he could chase you again."

Kayo and Rosie didn't know what to say.

"I acted against my own good judgment," Mr. Cookson said, "because I wanted to keep my son out of prison. Now I know I can't do that for him; he has to do it himself. It was a relief when I learned that the police caught Bert at the airport, even though I know he'll be locked up again."

Mr. Cookson stood up. "I'll go now," he said. "I just came to apologize, and to say goodbye."

"Goodbye?" Mrs. Tallie said. "You'll be here in the morning, won't you? Nine o'clock, as usual?"

"You want me to continue to work here, after what happened?"

"You made a mistake," Mrs. Tallie said, "but you're still the best gardener I've ever seen. It would be foolish of me not to keep you on, if you're willing to stay."

"Willing!" Mr. Cookson cried. "I'm more than willing. Thank you, Mrs. Tallie. I don't deserve this."

"There's just one condition," Mrs. Tallie said.

"You have your job as long as you don't chase my darling Muffin out of the flower beds. She's had enough trauma."

"I've put up with that fool cat all these years," Mr. Cookson said. "I suppose I can put up with her a while longer."

"Then it's settled," Mrs. Tallie said.

On their way home in the car, Rosie said, "One thing still bothers me. We didn't call the police, so why did they come to Mrs. Tallie's house?"

"Her attorney called them," Mrs. Saunders said. "He received a letter from Mrs. Tallie and grew concerned about her. Mr. Cookson called them, too, after Bert chased you, and agreed to meet them at Mrs. Tallie's house and give himself up."

"I never liked Mr. Cookson, but I feel sorry for him," Kayo said.

"There's a good chance he'll get a suspended sentence," Mrs. Saunders said. "It's his first offense, and he came forward voluntarily and admitted his part."

"What about Bert?" Kayo asked. "Will he get a suspended sentence?"

"Bert will spend many years in prison," Mrs. Saunders said.

Don't Go Near Mrs. Tallie

"Good," said Rosie. "Bert is unscrupulous."
She made a check in her notebook and then said,
"That's five times today."

"Now that Muffin has a home again," Kayo
said, "Care Club needs a new project."

"Your Care Club projects are giving me
frightmares," Mrs. Saunders said. "Can't you
girls take up stamp collecting?"

Sammy Hulenback was riding his bike up and
down the street in front of Rosie's house when
they got home. As the girls got out of the car, he
waved a piece of paper at them.

"Isn't that nice?" said Mrs. Saunders. "He
wrote his letter of apology already."

"Do we have to read it?" Rosie said.

"If Sammy was willing to write and apologize,"
Mrs. Saunders said, "you most certainly do have
to read his letter."

Rosie and Kayo trudged up the stairs to Rosie's room as Rosie unfolded Sammy's piece of
paper.

"Oh, no," she groaned. "It *is* another poem."

"Read it silently and then throw it away,"
Kayo said.

"It's addressed to both of us. If I have to read
it, you have to listen."

129

"Oh, all right. Let's get it over with."
Rosie took a deep breath and began to read:

"You told me I could keep the cat,
    And then you said to give it back."

"Wait a minute," Kayo said. "Cat and back
don't rhyme."
"Tell that to Sammy." Rosie continued:

"About your club. Here's what I meant:
    I'll join and be the president."

"Strike three!" Kayo cried. She grabbed the
piece of paper and tore it in half.
"There's a third verse," Rosie said. "Don't you
want to hear the end?"
"I will never," said Kayo, as she ripped his
poem into tiny pieces, "listen to another word of
Sammy's so-called poetry. President of Care
Club? Ha!" She threw the paper in Rosie's
wastebasket.
"Care Club's plan to find a home for Muffin
didn't end the way we thought it would," Rosie
said, as she got out her dictionary and began
looking for a new vocabulary word.

"It ended even better," said Kayo. "Muffin stays with Mrs. Tallie."

"For our next meeting," Rosie said, "let's groom our own pets and play with them. Bone Breath needs a bath and nothing scary can happen while we're combing our cats."

"Don't be too sure," said Kayo.

"I'm going to save Bone Breath's fur and knit a sweater with it," Rosie said.

"Let's save all the cat fur," said Kayo, "and knit a sweater for Bert."

About the Author

Peg Kehret's popular novels for young people are regularly nominated for state awards. She has received the Young Hoosier Award, the Golden Sower Award, the Iowa Children's Choice Award, the Celebrate Literacy Award, the Sequoyah Children's Book Award, and the Pacific Northwest Writers Conference Achievement Award. She lives with her husband, Carl, and their animal friends in Washington State, where she is a volunteer at the Humane Society and SPCA. Her two grown children and four grandchildren live in Washington, too.

Peg's Minstrel titles include *Nightmare Mountain; Sisters, Long Ago; Cages; Terror at the Zoo; Horror at the Haunted House;* and the *Frightmares*™ series.